JEDI QUEST

THE WAY OF THE APPRENTICE

JEDI QUEST

CHOSEN BY FATE.
DESTINED FOR CONFLICT.

#1 THE WAY OF THE APPRENTICE

#2 THE TRAIL OF THE JEDI

SPECIAL HARDCOVER EDITION: PATH TO TRUTH

. . . AND MORE TO COME

JEDI QUEST

BY JUDE WATSON

THE WAY OF THE APPRENTICE

SCHOLASTIC INC.

New York   Toronto   London   Auckland   Sydney
Mexico City   New Delhi   Hong Kong   Buenos Aires

www.starwars.com
www.starwarskids.com
www.scholastic.com

ISBN 0-439-33917-0

Cover art by Alicia Buelow and David Mattingly.

12 11 10 9 8 7 6 5 4 3   2 3 4 5 6 7/0

Printed in the U.S.A.
First Scholastic printing, May 2002

Not in living memory — not even among the oldest Jedi Masters — could they remember a Padawan who was as gifted as Anakin Skywalker. He could have advanced through his Temple training in half the time it had taken him. From the beginning, he had been far beyond his classmates in lightsaber skills and mastery of the Force. Yet in matters of the heart and mind, he still had much to learn, as Yoda continually pointed out.

His teachers had known how gifted he was, but they gave him the same drills and assignments as the other students. They knew he was bored at times, but it was important not to single him out, not to treat him as special.

But Anakin was special, and they all knew it. The trouble was that he knew it as well.

He had been a unique case from the moment he entered Jedi training at the Temple. For one thing, he had been allowed to enter despite having passed the usual age. For another, he had been chosen as a Padawan by Obi-Wan Kenobi from the start. While the other students wondered when they would be chosen, and by whom, Anakin's destiny was assured.

Obi-Wan watched Anakin's progress with an eye that was both loving and careful. In one hand he held Qui-Gon's faith; in the other he held Yoda's caution. There were times it was hard to balance these two powerful influences.

On the morning of Anakin's thirteenth birthday, Obi-Wan had presented him with his Padawan gift. It was the gift that Qui-Gon had given Obi-Wan on his own thirteenth birthday, a Force-sensitive river stone. Obi-Wan was ashamed to remember how he'd been disappointed by the gift. He had been so young. He had wanted something significant, something like the gifts other Padawans had received — special hilts for their lightsabers or cloaks made from the lightweight, warm wool from the planet Pasmin. Instead, Qui-Gon had given him a rock.

Yet that present had turned into his most valuable possession. The smooth black stone glowed with heat against his heart. It had warmed his cold hands on many planets. It had nestled inside a tiny pocket his friend Bant had sewn in his tunic, close to his heart.

It was hard to give it up. But somehow he knew Qui-Gon would want him to.

Unlike Obi-Wan's first reaction, Anakin's face showed deep appreciation. Then his expression clouded. "Are you sure?" he asked. "This was given to you by Qui-Gon."

"He would want you to have it, as I do. It is my most treasured possession." Obi-Wan reached out and closed Anakin's fingers over the stone. "I hope it will be with you always to remind you of Qui-Gon and me, of our deep regard for you."

Anakin's smile lit his face. "I'll treasure it. Thank you, Master."

In many ways, Anakin was more openhearted, more generous than he had once been, Obi-Wan thought. Though there was a great weight on Anakin due to the prophecy, he was sure that Anakin would do well.

Now Anakin was fourteen. He was an able Padawan who had already proven himself on several important missions. Yet there was one thing that nagged at Obi-Wan. Anakin was liked by the other students, but he had no close friends. He was not loved.

Obi-Wan told himself that Anakin's gifts naturally set him apart. But in his heart, he grieved for Anakin's lone-

liness. He was happy for Anakin's skill and growing command of the Force. But he wished a simple thing for Anakin. It was something he could not give his Padawan. It was not a gift he could hand over, like a well-loved river stone. He wished for a friend.

CHAPTER ONE

Anakin made his way down an alley deep below the gleaming surface of Coruscant. His Padawan braid was tucked inside his tunic, his lightsaber hidden in the folds of his cloak. The Jedi were treated with great respect everywhere on Coruscant — except here. Close to the planet's surface, there were those who matched their contempt for good society with their need to hide from it. Everyone was equal here. Equally despised.

Even air taxis didn't descend this far. It had taken him over an hour to walk down the descending ramps, since the lift tubes were often nonfunctional. If only he had an airspeeder! Then these raids could be done in half the time. But Jedi students didn't have access to their own speeders. Not even Padawans. Technically, he wasn't supposed to be outside the Temple at all, not without Obi-Wan's permission.

"Technically" is just another way of saying you are breaking the rules, Obi-Wan would say. *Either you obey a rule, or you do not.*

He was devoted to his Master, yet sometimes Obi-Wan's earnestness could really get in the way. Anakin didn't believe in breaking Jedi rules. He just wanted to find the spaces between them.

Anakin was well aware that his Master knew of these midnight jaunts. Obi-Wan was amazingly perceptive. He could sense a shift in emotion or thought faster than an eyeblink. Thank the moon and stars that Obi-Wan also preferred not to hear about his midnight trips. As long as Anakin was discreet and didn't get into trouble, Obi-Wan would turn a blind eye.

Anakin didn't want to trouble Obi-Wan, but he couldn't help himself. As the night wore on and the Temple quieted, as the Jedi students turned off their glow rods and settled down for night meditation and sleep, Anakin just got restless. The lure of the streets called him. There were projects he had to complete, droids he was building or refining, parts to scavenge, rusty treasures to uncover. But mostly he just needed to be outside, under the stars.

Only those of us who have been slaves can really taste freedom, he sometimes thought.

His favorite scavenger heap was down here, in the dark underbelly of the city. The glow lights were seldom repaired and the glittering lights of the city above didn't penetrate down this far. This was where the junk dealers dumped their unwanted heaps — the stuff even they couldn't sell. It was left in smoking, stinking gray piles for the lowest of the low to pick over.

Fights often erupted at these scavenger heaps. Anakin had been lucky to avoid the squabbles that could end in violence. In addition to the desperate, there were bands of Manikons, a tribe from a planet lost long ago to a civil war so devastating it had caused the small band of survivors to flee to Coruscant. Now the Manikons survived by their wits and their weapons. They were perfectly willing to fight to the death over a rusty hydrospanner.

Anakin slipped among the smoky piles. Normally he avoided this particular junkyard, but he had a difficult tech problem with a malfunctioning droid, and he had exhausted all his other venues for finding what he needed. He knew that his Master looked at his tinkering with droids and tech devices as a waste of his time. Maybe it was. Anakin didn't care. He had come to realize that he needed to occupy his mind in order to stop the voices in his head. The voices that doubted he'd ever be a great Jedi Knight. The voices that told him he'd abandoned his mother. . . .

Anakin shook his head. Working on the droids was the one slender thread that connected him to his childhood on Tatooine. It was a frayed thread he was not willing to snap off completely.

The smell came to his nostrils, a mixture of smoky metal and something unpleasantly organic, the residue of food or waste. He tuned it out as his gaze eagerly swept the rubble.

He was grateful for his Jedi training. His eyes were sharp, even in the shadows. He did not want to risk a glow rod. It was dangerous to advertise your presence here. Better to act as a shadow.

He kept his eyes trained on the ground as he walked. Sometimes parts dropped off the giant hydro-lifts that were used to transport the junk. He had uncovered some great finds by kicking through the dirt and debris beneath his boots.

Ah — a circuit, almost completely intact. Anakin rubbed it against his tunic, not caring about the crusty dirt that left a dark stain. He tucked it in his belt. And here — part of a hydrospanner. He could always use that, just in case he broke the ones he had. Cheaper to fuse an old one than to look for an intact one.

He scanned the heap ahead of him. One of his goals was to assemble his own small power terminal in his room so that he would not have to hook up to the Temple's terminal in order to power his droids. The more he stayed out of sight with his hobby, the better.

There — he could see it on top of the heap. Could it be a motivator circuit board? Yes — if he could just manage to Force-jump up there without sending the assembled heap of junk tumbling. He scanned the side of the heap for a good landing site. A battered piece of durasteel seemed to rest solidly on the junk beneath it. If he landed softly, he should be able to balance on it long enough to swipe the piece. He was a Jedi, and his balance was perfect. Anakin jumped.

He landed a bit harder than he had meant to, and with a little too much pressure on his right foot.

You're not a Jedi yet.

He heard Obi-Wan's gentle, admonishing tone in his ear even as he scrambled to avoid sending a small avalanche of parts back down the pile along with him.

Willing his muscles to stay flexible and his mind focused, he balanced carefully on the durasteel and eased out one hand . . .

. . . only to see another hand appear from the other side of the heap, reaching for the same part. No doubt it was a Manikon.

He wasn't about to let one Manikon come between him and a new motivator. Anakin threw himself forward, but he miscalculated how stable his footing was. Part of the heap began to slide, taking him along with it. He felt something or someone grab his ankle.

He crashed backward, at the same time reaching out to grab at the creature holding him. He felt some fabric in his fingers and held on. Together, the two of them banged and slid down the heap. Anakin smashed against sharp objects and bumped against durasteel and chunks of ferrocrete, still furiously hanging on to the scrap of fabric while his ankle was held securely in the creature's grasp.

At last they hit bottom. Anakin wrenched his foot away and sprang to his feet, ready for battle. The other creature did the same.

The hood of the creature fell back, and Anakin found himself face-to-face with a fellow Jedi student, Tru Veld.

"What are you doing here?" Anakin hissed angrily.

"That was my part," Tru answered. "I had my hand right on it."

"I was reaching for it —"

"And thanks to you, it's lost now."

Suddenly Anakin spotted the part on the ground between them. It must have slid down along with them. He pounced on it.

"It's not lost now!" he cried, grinning.

"Give that to me, Anakin," Tru said, his slanted silver eyes gleaming. Tru was a humanoid species, a native of the planet Teevan. His skin had a silvery cast, and he was tall and lanky. Teevans were exceptionally flexible and could bend in surprising ways. Anakin suddenly remembered that this quality had made Tru very good at fighting.

"I'm not afraid of you," Anakin said.

"Of course you're not," Tru said in a disgusted tone. "I'm not going to fight you for it. I'm waiting for you to do the right thing."

Anakin frowned. There were times he forgot he was a Jedi. For a moment, he had been the slave boy on Tatooine, still bound by the rules of play on that harsh world. *Those who find, keep. Those who hesitate, lose.*

He wasn't a slave boy. He was a Jedi.

"I have a Protocol Droid with a bad motivator," Anakin said. "I really need this."

But Tru wasn't listening. He was squinting into the darkness. "Now we're in for it," he said in a low tone. He signaled to Anakin. A short distance away, Anakin saw a clump of moving shapes. Manikons.

"If we're very quiet," Anakin murmured, "they won't spot us." He took a step back, and his foot kicked a piece of durasteel scrap. It landed against another piece of junk with a loud clang.

"Is that what you call quiet?" Tru hissed.

The Manikons turned. They saw the Jedi.

"Maybe if we don't move, they won't come at us," Anakin breathed.

The Manikons surged forward.

"Interesting notion," Tru said. "Got any other ideas?"

CHAPTER TWO

Manikons ran on four legs and reared up to two when attacking. They had blunt, heavy feet that they used to bludgeon their enemy. If they got close, they could spew a stinging venom from their eyes that had the power to temporarily blind their attacker.

There was no question that Anakin and Tru would need their lightsabers. Before the thought had completely registered, Anakin found the hilt in his hand. He didn't think it was such a good idea to reveal the fact that two Jedi were scavenging beneath the city. But he didn't particularly want to be pummeled and blinded, either.

Tru jumped to his left, and Anakin immediately saw his strategy. He wanted to avoid the pummeling feet and the stinging venom, which could only be directed straight ahead. Anakin followed Tru, leaping to engage the first Manikon. He knew he was a more aggressive fighter than Tru. He needed to avoid wounding or killing. He just had to frighten the Manikons enough to retreat.

"If we attack their bundles, they'll retreat," he told Tru confidently. "They won't want to lose what they have."

He leaped forward, going after the booty tied to their backs in large sacks. Whirling and dodging the flying feet, he slashed at the straps of leather tying the bags to their backs. The maneuver required the most precise of touches. A fraction off, and he could easily slice off an arm. This was why he loved the action of a lightsaber. It was the ultimate instrument. He had seen firsthand the mistake that many Jedi students made. They did not realize how delicate it could be, how you could use it like a breath of air. *Like a feather, not a stick,* the best lightsaber teacher, Soara Antana, had said.

Three bundles fell, scattering parts, and the Manikons howled in rage. They leaped over the parts and thundered toward Anakin and Tru.

Fffffeewwwww!

Anakin had never heard the sound of a Manikon spewing venom before, but he didn't need a lesson.

"Whoa, really good plan, Anakin," Tru observed.

Anakin leaped to his right as a snarling Manikon approached, rearing up on two legs. Tru rushed forward and delivered a fast series of moves to push back the Manikon.

"Okay, time," Tru said.

"Time for what?"

"New plan. Run."

"Good idea." Anakin took off after Tru.

The two of them leaped together, using the Force to help them gain the top of the junk heap in one bound. They sent a shower of debris down behind them, but they managed to keep their footing.

Below, the snarling Manikons began to scale the heap in their fury. But they were heavier and clumsier than the Jedi. The junk heap began to tumble and sway.

Anakin looked over at Tru.

"What now?"

"Jump?" Tru suggested.

"Sure. Any suggestions where?" They were surrounded by other junk heaps, all of them unstable. It was impossible to know if they would be able to land safely.

A huge Manikon was halfway up the slope when he dislodged a power converter fragment. The entire heap began to collapse.

"Anywhere!" Tru yelled, and leaped into the air.

Anakin followed. In midair, he had a second to decide on his landing spot. If he hadn't had Jedi training, chances were good that he would have landed on a spike or sharp piece of metal. But he was able to evaluate and direct his descent, even as he fell. Everything below him was suddenly sharp, suddenly clear. He felt he could see every pebble, every grain of dirt and debris. That was how clear the Force could make his vision.

It was moments like this that he lived for. The night air, so crisp in his lungs. Danger so near. The Force around him. If he could hang in the air forever like this, he would.

He landed lightly, precisely, on the edge of a heap, then jumped the rest of the way to the ground. Beside him, Tru landed safely as well.

Fffffeewwwwww!

Anakin jumped, pulling Tru aside. The venom hit only millimeters away.

They looked behind them. Three furious Manikons were trying to slide down the heap toward them. Junked parts were shifting and sliding.

"Time to go," Tru panted.

They ran. Behind them, the enormous junk heap collapsed in a cloud of dust. The cry of the Manikons was terrible. Choking, Anakin and Tru kept running. They didn't stop until they reached the relative safety of the walkway.

They paused to catch their breath. It had been a close call.

They struck off in the direction of the lift ramp to the upper levels of Coruscant.

"Well, if you say so," Tru said.

Anakin looked at him, confused. "If I say what?"

"Your droid has a bad motivator," Tru explained. "What makes you think so?"

"The reactivate switch keeps cutting out. This is my second motivator. The first one just blew when I hooked it up. I spent two weeks rebuilding it, too."

"Then your problem isn't the motivator," Tru said. "Have you run a check on the sensory plug-in system?"

Anakin shook his head. "Nothing wrong with it."

"Maybe. But sometimes it can interface with the re-activate switch and cause the motivator to fuse. Did something funny happen with the vocabulator when the first motivator blew?"

"That's funny," Anakin said. "It went crazy. My droid started talking in Kyhhhsik."

"That's your problem, then," Tru said. "The sensor suite has a short. Sometimes in Protocol Droids it can trigger the vocabulator. It's a pretty simple problem to fix. Much more simple than a bad motivator."

Anakin glanced at Tru's tall, gangly body. Tru had never impressed him. Sometimes Anakin had wondered if his connection to the Force was strong enough to be a Jedi. Yet Tru had recently been picked as a Padawan by Ry-Gaul, a quiet and respected Jedi Knight. Anakin had wondered about that, too.

"I didn't know you knew so much about droids," Anakin said.

"I don't. I just picked up a few things along the way," Tru said. "I like to read manuals in my spare time. Droids. Transports. Circuit boards. You name it."

Anakin tossed him the motivator part. "Here. I guess I won't need this after all."

Tru tucked it into the pocket of his tunic. "Thanks."

"That is, if you're right," Anakin added.

"If I'm not, you can have the part back."

Suddenly, Anakin began to understand why Tru had been picked by Ry-Gaul. There was the sense of assurance Tru had. He gave off a sense of calm. That was unusual in a young student, even a Jedi. Anakin himself was aware that he felt confused and uncertain some of the time. He covered it well. But Tru didn't seem to have an undercurrent. He was just Tru.

"Give me a summary when you're done with the analysis," Tru said.

"Of the droid?" Anakin asked.

"Of me," Tru answered. "Aren't you analyzing me right now?"

Anakin grinned and didn't bother to deny it. "I haven't come to any conclusions yet."

Tru took a bag of sweet figda candy from his pocket and tossed one to Anakin. "Too bad living beings don't come with manuals. Listen, I'm not very mechanical, but I'll help you with your droid problem, if you want."

Anakin was surprised at the offer, but he wasn't sure why. Then he realized what it was.

It wasn't often that he was offered help.

Most assumed he didn't need it.

"Sure," Anakin said. Saying that one word opened a door. He saw that suddenly. He had forgotten it. He had once known how to make a friend, and he had made friends easily. It was a skill he had lost.

His comlink signaled, and he groaned. He knew who it was.

"Where are you?" Obi-Wan asked.

Anakin looked around. He was still quite a few levels away from the Temple. At least a few hundred. If he told his Master that, Obi-Wan would know where he'd been, and why.

Tru suddenly stepped up closer. "Master Kenobi, it is Tru Veld. Anakin is with me. I asked his help on . . . a personal matter. We are returning to the Temple now."

"All right." Obi-Wan sounded surprised. "Come and see me, Anakin, as soon as you arrive."

Anakin turned off his comlink. "Thanks," he said to Tru. "Obi-Wan wouldn't be happy if he knew where I'd been."

"Neither would Ry-Gaul," Tru said.

"If you're not so good at fixing droids, why were you there?" Anakin asked.

"I'm helping out Ali Alann," Tru said. "He has a droid helper in the nursery now. It needs a new motivator and the tech service department is running low. I thought I'd surprise him."

Anakin felt ashamed. Here he had fought for the part for himself, and Tru was doing a good deed. He sighed. It was times such as this he wondered if he'd ever become a Jedi. Students like Tru had a dedication he feared he lacked.

They hurried back to the Temple. It was dark and quiet as they checked in. They headed for the lift tube.

Obi-Wan came around the corner. He frowned when he saw Anakin's stained tunic and dirty face.

"Where have you been?" he asked sternly.

Tru and Anakin looked at each other, then began to speak at once.

"You see, Ali Alann —" Tru began.

"The tech service department has shortages —" Anakin started.

Obi-Wan held up a hand. "I don't want to know. Good night, Tru."

Tru nodded respectfully and hurried off to his quarters. Obi-Wan turned back to Anakin.

"Anakin, these late hours will do you no good if you have to leave early on a mission the next day."

"But I don't have a mission tomorrow," Anakin said.

"Ah. Are you so certain of that, young Padawan? Do you see into the minds of the Jedi Council?"

"The Jedi Council wants to see us," Anakin guessed, excitement rising in him. "You mean we have a mission?"

"We shall see," Obi-Wan said neutrally. "They've asked for our presence before dawn tomorrow. So get some sleep. If I see one yawn tomorrow, I'll forbid you to go outside the Temple grounds at all."

CHAPTER THREE

The next morning, Obi-Wan headed for Anakin's quarters. He knew that Anakin would be ready at the precise time he had been told. Anakin might push the rules, but he knew when to toe the line.

Anakin was waiting outside his door in a fresh tunic, his face bright with eagerness in the dim light. The glow rods were kept low at this hour to keep a meditative hush in the Temple halls. Most Jedi were asleep or meditating.

Anakin swung into step beside him. Obi-Wan knew that his Padawan was waiting for an admonishment about the night before, but Obi-Wan had already moved on. The sight of Anakin with Tru had stirred him. The two young Padawans had exchanged a conspiratorial glance, and rather than being nettled by it, Obi-Wan had enjoyed it — though he would never let Anakin know it. Perhaps Anakin had made a friend.

Obi-Wan was also glad that Anakin had an independent spirit. It would serve him well as a Jedi Knight in the years to come. What his Padawan needed was training in cooperation and dedication to the greater good, upheld by the Jedi Order. He did not know how to suppress his own needs and desires in order to serve. *How does one teach loyalty and self-sacrifice?* Obi-Wan wondered. Was it something that *could* be taught?

The mission teaches when I cannot.

Qui-Gon's words again. Obi-Wan had come to realize that in addition to preparing him to be a Jedi Knight, Qui-Gon had prepared him to be a Master as well. He had often let him in on his thought processes, even on his own struggles to be a good Master. Qui-Gon's advice often rose in his mind, centering and calming him, much as Qui-Gon himself had done.

Over the years since Qui-Gon's tragic death, Obi-Wan had come to know how even searing grief could leave behind not only sorrow, but peace. It had been one of the great lessons of his life.

"You are thinking of Qui-Gon." Anakin's voice was soft.

Startled, Obi-Wan turned to his Padawan. "How did you know?"

"Your face. It changes." Anakin shrugged. "Some knot inside you loosens. Something smooths out. I see it happening."

"Stop being so perceptive," Obi-Wan chided gently.

"Now you are not thinking of him at all," Anakin replied, mischief in his eyes. "The knot is back."

"And you have tied it," Obi-Wan answered, accessing the Council room door.

The full Council had not yet assembled. Only Yoda and Mace Windu were present, speaking quietly by the window. The lights of Coruscant still sparkled outside. The sun had not yet risen. A few air taxis made their way down the space lanes. In only an hour or so those lanes would be crammed with traffic.

Obi-Wan was surprised to see two other Jedi Knights in the room with their Padawans. Obviously this mission was going to be a big one. He gave short bows to Ry-Gaul and Soara Antana. Ry-Gaul's Padawan was Tru Veld, Anakin's companion of the night before. The tall, elegant Master towered over his Padawan. Obi-Wan did not know Ry-Gaul very well, though he knew his reputation. He was a grave, silent Jedi who did not speak much but was widely respected for the depth of his knowledge of the galaxy. Soara Antana was a legend. Her lightsaber skills had set her apart even as a young girl. Like Obi-Wan, she had recently become a Jedi

Knight. Her Padawan, Darra Thel-Tanis, was the same age as Anakin. Darra, a slender girl with lively eyes, took her place next to the sturdy, muscular Soara.

The Jedi Council members filed in and took their places. Yoda and Mace Windu came away from the window and sat. They exchanged a glance but did not start the proceedings. What were they waiting for?

The doors hissed open again, and Siri strode in. Obi-Wan hid his smile. He should have known. When he had known Siri as a young Padawan, she had been strict about rules and regulations. But ever since she had gone undercover to trap the slave pirate Krayn, he had noticed a difference in her. She seemed a little restless, less inclined to listen wholeheartedly to the Council. Obi-Wan didn't mind the change. Siri had always seemed just a bit too inflexible. Now she even looked like a rebel. Her blond hair was cropped short, unlike the other Jedi Masters. Instead of a tunic and cloak, she wore a close-fitting unisuit made of leather. She nodded at him and took her place next to her Padawan, Ferus Olin.

Mace Windu's stern gaze swept over them all. "Thank you all for your punctuality," he said, giving Siri a pointed look that only caused her chin to lift and her lips to quirk in a small, apologetic smile. "We have an emergency mission that requires the service of four

Jedi teams. You are to travel to Radnor, a planet overcome by a toxic disaster. Radnor is a small planet known for its research and development of high-tech weapons systems. A toxic cloud has been accidentally released by one of their weapons laboratories and is quickly spreading. Many have died; many more have become ill. So far the damage has been confined to one area."

"Two main city-states there are on Radnor," Yoda said. "Twin cities, they are called. Tacto and Aubendo. Small cities they are, each with their own governing ministers. Prevailing winds they have on Radnor. The winds sent the toxic cloud directly to Aubendo. Confined there the toxin has been. Yet no one knows exactly how it has spread."

"Since it is a new agent, there are many unknowns. It could be ingested into the lungs or through the skin," Mace Windu continued. "The agent is not a gas, but an organic substance carried by the air. It could possibly be spread from one being to another — we don't know this, either. The second city of Tacto has been spared as of yet."

"Change the prevailing wind will," Yoda said. "Then bring it will the toxin to the second city."

"At first Radnor dealt admirably with the disaster,"

Mace went on. "The officials mobilized quickly to meet the catastrophe. The afflicted city of Aubendo and the surrounding area was cordoned off and is now called the Isolation Sector. Tacto is known as the Clear Sector, and there have been no cases so far. But as Tacto saw how severely afflicted Aubendo became, as they saw the numbers of deaths increase so that not one being was spared, they began to panic. The governing ministers of Tacto fled the planet. Anyone who could afford to joined them. There are now no more transports left on the planet to take those who could go. Anarchy and panic have taken over. So the Senate is stepping in. Evacuation vessels capable of transporting the remaining Tacto population are headed to Radnor and will arrive in three days."

"Surprised you look, Obi-Wan," Yoda observed.

"Merely that the Senate has acted so quickly," Obi-Wan said. Mired in bureaucracy, the Senate sometimes took months to debate a simple issue.

"Dire, the situation is," Yoda said, nodding. "Bail Organa was responsible for this quick action."

"There will be room for the sick as well as for those who haven't been exposed," Mace Windu went on. "But on the planet's surface there is panic among the healthy population, for they are afraid that there will not be enough room. Corrupt lower officials are taking bribes, so it is also feared that the sick will never make it off the planet at all."

"Chaos begun cannot be ordered so easily," Yoda said.

"You must go in and ensure that the evacuations take place in a peaceful and orderly manner," Mace said. "There are still those who survive in Aubendo, and their places on the evacuation ships must be assured. There is looting and unrest in Tacto, so the Jedi must keep the peace as well. It is a volatile situation that means life or death for many, so we have decided that four teams are needed."

"Transport you must medications to the sick on the planet," Yoda added. "And leave you must this morning."

"A Senate transport is waiting," Mace Windu concluded. "May the Force be with you."

CHAPTER FOUR

The Senate transport slid into orbit around Radnor. No transports were allowed to land on the planet. They would take a small cruiser to the surface.

Anakin stared down at the planet. From space, it looked blue-green, and he knew that vast seas covered much of the surface. The main landmass was small, and appeared as though the seas around it would swallow it up.

He had visited other worlds since he'd become a Padawan. It no longer surprised him when he saw planets whose surfaces were dominated by oceans and seas. As a boy, he could not imagine seas that could stretch as far as the eye could see. On Tattooine, he had lived in an ocean of sand.

"Hard to imagine, isn't it," Tru said, breaking into his thoughts. "When you look down at a planet, I mean."

"What?" Anakin asked.

"Suffering," Tru said. "Everything seems peaceful from orbit. Then you get down there, in the middle of things, and everything changes."

"How many missions have you been on?" Anakin asked.

"Enough," Tru said softly. "Enough to have seen what I've seen. Enough to know I will see more."

It sounded like a riddle. Yet, strangely, Anakin knew what he meant. Each mission made him feel so much older. Each mission had exposed him to sadness and anger and grief. Nevertheless he looked forward to the next, and the next. That was what Tru meant.

"This is my first mission." Darra Thel-Tanis spoke behind them. She had not said much on the journey, instead studying the research materials the Council had provided. She had lively, rust-colored eyes and a piece of bright fabric woven through her long Padawan braid. Her energy crackled. Anakin could almost feel it in the air when she was near. "So I'm depending on you two to make me look good." Darra gave Tru and Anakin a cheerful grin.

Obi-Wan came by and put a hand on Anakin's shoulder. "It's time to board the cruiser."

The four Jedi teams — Anakin and Obi-Wan, Tru and Ry-Gaul, Darra and Soara, and Ferus and Siri — made their way to the cargo bay. They settled into the cruiser and Siri took the controls.

Ferus Olin sat up front next to her, the light glinting off the streaks of gold in his thick dark hair. Anakin watched his profile. It was strictly emphasized in the Jedi Temple that no student was better than another. Different students had different gifts. Yet Ferus had them all. He was steady and brilliant, a physically gifted athlete, and popular with all the students. He was a few years older than Anakin, and the Masters were still talking about him long after he had gone on to become a Padawan.

He had excelled at everything he tried. Yet no student was jealous of him. They admired him and wanted to be like him. He was also popular with the Jedi Council. Anakin knew they expected great things of him. There was no one at the Temple who did not speak the name Ferus without praise.

Except for Anakin. There was something about Ferus he did not like. That was not appropriate, of course. It was not up to Anakin to like or dislike a student. Judgment was forbidden in the Jedi Order.

He tried to control the feeling. He *would* control it. He knew well that he couldn't be a Jedi without doing so.

Siri expertly maneuvered the craft down to the landing site at Tacto. She came in fast and whipped the craft around, landing with a whisper-light touch that Anakin admired. All Jedi were excellent pilots, but it was rare to find someone who approached the task as artfully as Siri.

"Great landing," Anakin told her. Obi-Wan just sighed.

Siri activated the landing ramp, and they filed down onto the surface of the planet. Ry-Gaul carried the case holding the needed medications. Anakin reached out to the Force to feel what he could about the mission ahead. He exchanged a glance with Obi-Wan. The Force was dark here. Fear had gripped the population of both cities — and with fear came desperation, anger, and chaos.

Radnorans were a humanoid species, short in stature and sturdy in appearance. Several uniformed security officers waited at the transport desk. A Radnoran dressed in a white unicoat hurried forward.

"Welcome, Jedi. We are relieved to see you. The city of Tacto is under great stress." He passed a hand over his head full of curly brown hair. "The people don't believe that there will be enough room on the ships."

"Who are you?" Soara Antana asked bluntly. She

was known for her no-nonsense approach. Her powerful hands rested lightly on her belt.

"Excuse me. I should explain. I am Galen, the coordinator of the rescue effort. The officials have abandoned the planet, so I suppose I'm now in charge. Only a small security force remains. I inherited this job — I'm normally a scientist. Most of my colleagues have left. I volunteered to help with the evacuation. My sister Curi has gone to the Isolation Sector to help there." Galen turned to the security officers. "Remain here with the Jedi ship."

The lead officer nodded. "Affirmative."

"Let me take you to the emergency command post," Galen said.

Galen started across the landing pad, taking quick steps with his short, muscular legs. "Rumors come and go daily. The ships are late. The ships are not coming. There will not be enough room. We try to keep information flowing, but it's difficult. So many have left, and those who remain are frightened."

"How are things in the Isolation Sector?" Soara Antana asked.

"Worse," Galen said curtly. "Communication is erratic. The toxic cloud has apparently interfered with our comm systems. We —"

Suddenly, they heard the roar of engines. They turned just in time to see their transport lift off the landing pad and zoom high above.

Galen turned to them, his round, ruddy face suddenly pale. "The security officers stole your ship. I am so sorry. Things here are very bad. Even the officers are panicking. Why shouldn't they? Everyone else is, and their own leader has fled. But don't worry — I have a transport in a safe location. It is at your disposal."

"We accept your offer with thanks," Siri said.

"We can go there after you see the command post," Galen said, beginning to walk again.

"We can assure your people that the ships are on their way and there is room for all. What is your biggest problem at the moment?" Obi-Wan asked.

"I have too many problems to single out one," Galen said. "The government is practically nonexistent. The security officers — the ones who remain — are in danger of disbanding. You can see that loyalty has evaporated on Radnor."

They exited onto a boulevard and found themselves in the city center. The streets were eerily empty. Occasionally a Radnoran would pass, walking quickly. They saw a family go by, their bundles held tightly against their chests, darting glances testifying to their panic.

They passed looted stores and houses. Doors were

broken down and windows were smashed. Anyone they passed had at least one blaster prominently displayed on a hip or strapped across a chest.

Anakin had never seen anything like it. He could almost smell the fear in the air.

They walked by a small space cruiser, its interior bombed out and its engine looted.

"Most of the transports that have remained have been fought over and destroyed," Galen explained. "There have been frenzied crowds desperate to get off-planet."

"Tell us about the looters," Soara said. "Do you have any clues as to who they are and where they are based?"

"No," Galen said. "I don't have time to find out. At any rate, we don't have a security force to control them. I can tell you that the raiders have somehow stolen a small army of prototype Battle Droids from a research laboratory. They use the droids to control the situation while they steal the goods."

Galen's comlink signaled, and he answered it. After exchanging a few words, he turned to the Jedi. "It is my sister, Curi. I'd like you to see this."

A miniature hologram appeared of a small Radnoran female. They could just glimpse curly dark hair like Galen's beneath the white bio-isolation suit she wore.

Every inch of her body was covered, with the material stretching over her boots. A transparent mask fitted over her face and head. The hologram flickered, and some of the words were unclear.

". . . three deaths today of med personnel. There aren't enough of us to take care of . . . We need the new medications as soon as possible. Please tell the Jedi . . ."

The hologram sputtered and died.

The message might have been garbled, but the controlled panic in her voice was clear.

"We should head there immediately," Soara said.

"I can take you as far as the energy gate that divides the sectors," Galen told them. "It's not far. I can supply you with bio-isolation suits."

They came to a store guarded by several Radnorans with blasters. A sign in the window announced: BIO-ISO SUITS 5,000 KARSEMS.

"Five thousand karsems is a full year's salary," Galen remarked. "We are lucky to have suits for you. They are hidden. I don't keep them at the command center, because it's already been attacked by looters looking for suits."

Suddenly, they heard the sound of screams coming from the street ahead.

Galen looked nervous. "What now?"

The Jedi did not stop to wonder. Masters and Padawans charged ahead, running toward the source of the sound.

They rounded a corner. Ahead was a large, prosperous-looking house. Its windows had been hastily covered with durasteel panels. The door had been nailed shut with thick durasteel slabs crisscrossing it.

None of the attempts to make the house a fortress had worked. The door had been kicked in. Two of the windows had the durasteel torn away. Raiders were throwing goods out of the windows.

Twenty Battle Droids like none Anakin had ever seen were wheeling in formation. They had advanced repulsorlift systems, allowing them to move with astonishing speed above the surface of the ground. While they guarded a huddled group, Radnorans systematically loaded the looted goods onto gravsleds.

One Radnoran male lay on the ground in a spreading pool of blood. A female crouched over him. Children stood nearby, rooted to the spot, while another older female tried to herd them to safety.

Anakin saw all this at once. His gaze took in the number of droids, the number of raiders, the Radnorans who must be protected, and the possible angles of attack. He knew every Jedi had observed the same. The droids had a fluid movement he'd never seen before. They did not maneuver in a jerky, programmed fashion. It was almost as though they had grace built into their sensors, and their blaster accuracy ratio was much higher than the usual Battle Droid.

One of the Radnoran raiders spotted them. Anakin saw his fingers fly on a remote device clipped to his belt. Five of the droids moved to surround the raiders for protection. The rest wheeled and came straight toward the Jedi in attack formation.

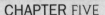

CHAPTER FIVE

"Padawans, protection!" Siri ordered crisply. Her words floated behind her; Siri was already Force-jumping toward the front line of droids.

Obi-Wan leaped as well, keeping to Siri's left so they could surround the droids, who were deftly moving over the ground. With one sweep of her lightsaber, Siri sliced a droid neatly in half. Simultaneously, Obi-Wan did the same to the second. On his backswing, he took out a third.

As quick and agile as Siri and Obi-Wan were, Soara Antana was even faster. Anakin watched in astonishment as her lightsaber cut through three droids with one clean stroke. Ry-Gaul handed the medication case to Tru to safeguard and joined her side.

Anakin knew that Siri's order was for the Padawans to surround the Radnoran family that had been victimized by the attackers. But he could see that the Jedi Masters would need help with the rest of the droids and the Radnoran raiders, who were already peppering them with blaster fire.

Darra, Tru, and Ferus raced to surround the Radnoran family. Ferus took out a droid on his way in a quick detour, his red lightsaber flashing. Anakin knew the three Padawans could easily follow through on Siri's order. That meant that on his way to obey Siri's order, he could help the Jedi Masters.

Anakin detoured toward Soara and Ry-Gaul. He held his lightsaber at the ready. The hilt he had built in a trance in the cave of Illum was perfectly balanced to his hand. He felt power surge through him.

Anakin took out two droids with two quick thrusts. His palms felt hot, his body strong, his timing sharp. Still, he lagged behind Ry-Gaul and the amazing Soara, whose compact body now seemed to move like molten metal, gracefully sliding from one attack position to another. Each of Soara's moves flowed into the next, with no beginning and no end. Her lightsaber was a blur as it sliced efficiently and continuously through one droid after another.

The Radnoran raiders took one look at how quickly

the Jedi had reduced most of their droid squad to a smoking heap. They ran.

The rest of the droids closed in to protect the raider's retreat. Anakin saw quickly that the Jedi Masters had the situation in hand. He double-flipped back to join the other Padawans, who had formed a tight circle, their backs to the Radnoran family as they fended off the last of the blaster fire from the retreating droids.

Ferus moved aside so that Anakin could join the protective circle. Anakin kept his lightsaber moving, deflecting the fire as the family crouched behind him.

Four of the droids suddenly peeled off into one group and launched a frontal attack on Obi-Wan, taking him momentarily by surprise. Siri had to execute a reversal and come at them from behind. Anakin admired how well Obi-Wan and Siri seemed to anticipate each other's strategy in combating the droids' sudden maneuver.

That was not the only surprise. While Obi-Wan and Siri battled the group of droids, three more separated from the rest and suddenly zoomed toward the Radnoran family.

"Watch it!" Ferus called.

"I see it," Anakin muttered, his teeth clenched. Ferus spoke as though he'd been the only one to catch the surprise attack.

Tru turned his body so that he was still protecting the Radnorans and the case in his left hand but could meet the droid attack head on. Darra switched her lightsaber from her right hand to her left. All Jedi were trained to use both hands while fighting, but Darra was especially skilled at not favoring one over the other.

Ferus stepped forward, and Anakin did the same. The two Padawans fought the three droids side by side. It took all their powers to stay ahead of them.

Anakin saw a droid come at Ferus's left, and moved to foil its approach at the same time as Ferus. The two Padawans collided, sending Ferus off balance. He landed awkwardly, and Anakin quickly rushed in to bury his lightsaber in the droid's control center. Ferus was up and fighting in another split second, his eyebrows furrowed in concentration. He sliced a droid in two as Darra dispatched the last one with a cool grace Anakin admired.

Anakin glanced over at Obi-Wan. He was ready to join his Master, but he saw that Obi-Wan and Siri had finished off the rest of the droids. Soara and Ry-Gaul had completed their work as well.

The Jedi simultaneously deactivated their light-sabers. Obi-Wan ran to the Radnoran family.

"Is anyone badly hurt?" he asked.

"My husband," the Radnoran female said, her eyes wide with panic. "He needs help."

"We'll get him to a medic," Tru assured her.

Ry-Gaul bent over the Radnoran to gently examine the wound. "He will be all right. He needs a bacta bath." It was rare for Ry-Gaul to say so much at once.

"My sister took a blow to the head," the man's wife said, pointing at the older Radnoran female.

"And you," Tru said gently. He touched her shoulder. "You have taken a blow yourself, I think."

"To the leg. It was nothing," the wife said, kneeling by her husband.

"They all need care," Tru said to Ry-Gaul.

"Yes," Obi-Wan said. He scanned the streets. "There are no speeder transports. No emergency med vehicles."

As if he'd heard them, suddenly Galen appeared, piloting a large speeder. "I thought you might need this here."

"Yes. We must transport the wounded," Soara said. "And then we must go to the Isolation Sector."

"I can take the wounded first, then return for you," Galen said. "By the way, I only have four bio-isolation suits. You will have to choose who will go."

The four Masters exchanged glances. They did not

have to confer. It would be better to leave the Padawans here temporarily and not expose them to the deadly toxin. The Masters were sure to be back in time to monitor the evacuations.

"The Padawans will stay here and make sure the wounded get care," Soara said, speaking for all the Masters. "We shall bring the medications to the Isolation Sector."

"Your instructions are to patrol the area and keep the people as calm as possible," Obi-Wan told the Padawans. "Do not conceal your lightsabers. The Radnorans must know that the Jedi will protect them."

"Check in with Galen periodically," Siri said. "He'll keep up with the progress of the evacuation ships."

"We will not fail you," Ferus said.

Of course we won't. You don't need to say it, Anakin thought.

Obi-Wan drew Anakin aside. "You fought well, my young Padawan," he told him.

"Thank you, Master."

"But you fought for yourself," Obi-Wan continued. "First of all, you did not obey Siri's order at once. And when Ferus stepped forward to engage the droids, he did so in the expectation that the two of you would work *together.* Instead, you fought as though you were fighting alone. You will never be a great Jedi warrior if you do not practice teamwork and dedicate yourself to the greater Jedi goal."

It was his Master's most disapproving tone. Anakin knew better than to try to defend himself. Hadn't Ferus fought for himself, too? Hadn't he stepped forward without consulting Anakin, without a word as to his intentions? Why was Ferus right, and he wrong?

"Yes, Master," he said.

Obi-Wan stepped back. He never said more than he needed to. He never added a reassurance after a correction.

Anakin turned away. He caught Ferus's eye, and the boy quickly looked away. Ferus had overheard Obi-Wan! Anakin's face burned. Now Ferus knew that Anakin had been corrected by his Master. And Ferus was about the last Padawan in the Jedi Order that Anakin would want to know that.

The others had loaded the wounded into the speeder. There was just enough room for the Padawans.

"I'll return for you," Galen said to the Jedi Masters before taking off. Anakin watched as they receded behind him. He knew it was important for them to get the wounded to a medic. He also knew the Masters had left them here temporarily with important responsibilities. He still wished he were going off with his Master to see the Isolation Sector. Someday he would be a Jedi Master. Then he would be the one to make decisions, the one to make corrections. He could hardly wait.

CHAPTER SIX

Galen picked up the Jedi Masters and brought them to the boundary line of the Clear Sector. An energy gate was ahead.

"I'll enter the code, and you'll be able to pass through," Galen said. "I'm sorry I can't give you the transport, but no vehicle can pass through the energy gate. You'll have to put on your bio-iso suits. I've managed to get a message through to Curi. You should be met on the other side for transport to Aubendo."

"Thank you for all your help," Obi-Wan said. He gave a last look back at Tacto. Obi-Wan didn't second-guess decisions, but he suddenly wished Anakin were with him.

The Jedi donned the bio-iso suits. The energy gate blinked green, and they walked through. They stood on a vast plain. There was only a smudge of gray on the horizon, an indication of the city ahead.

After a few moments they saw a transport approaching. They recognized Galen's sister as the Radnoran female who was piloting the craft.

She halted the craft near them, the repulsorlift engines keeping it slightly aloft. "You've brought the medication?"

Ry-Gaul indicated the case at his side. "Here."

"Thank the stars. Oh, I'm so sorry. What a way to greet you. I am Curi. I extend so many thanks to the Jedi for coming. Please board the craft."

The Jedi swung themselves into the airspeeder. As Curi took off, they introduced themselves.

"I'm in charge of the rescue operation here, such as it is," Curi said. "We are fighting a battle we cannot win."

"You have many fatalities?" Obi-Wan asked.

Curi gave him a bleak look, full of exhaustion and suffering. "Everyone in this sector is dead or dying. Only those who came in from the Clear Sector with bio-iso suits are healthy."

The gray towers of the city rose before them. "We're almost there," Curi said. "We are passing over the underground canyons now."

Below them, the ground was fissured with deep

cracks that Obi-Wan could see led to a maze of canyons.

"Radnorans are city dwellers," Curi explained. "We do not like open spaces. Perhaps some of us could have escaped the toxin if we weren't all in the same place."

They reached the outskirts of the city. Curi slowed down as they went down a wide boulevard. It was deserted. Abandoned air taxis littered the street in haphazard groups. Cafes and businesses were shuttered and empty.

There was no one on the streets. It was as though the Radnorans of this city had vanished. Obi-Wan had expected to see signs of panic, but the buildings and surroundings were intact.

Everything would have seemed almost normal, except for the fact that there wasn't any sign of a living thing. Even the vegetation was dead. Flower beds were full of twisted stalks. A massive tree was bare of leaves, the spiky branches reaching out like pleading arms. They could see that once-flowering bushes meters tall had run down the center strip of the wide boulevard. Now dry leaves and blooms were kicked up by the wind.

The Jedi were silent as they viewed the eerie sight. Obi-Wan had seen civil war and environmental disaster, but this felt worse. Even in his bio-iso suit, he imagined he could smell death in the air he breathed.

Ahead they saw the large med center. Here, at least, there were signs of activity. They could see medics in bio-iso suits inside the courtyard.

Curi pulled up the speeder, and they got out. The sound of his footsteps was unsettling to Obi-Wan. Encased in the white suit, his audio perception was muffled, making everything seem not quite real.

Curi hurried over to a medic and handed over the medications. "We don't know if these will help," she said to the Jedi. "We are trying anything. Thank you for bringing them."

She leaned against the wall, exhaustion showing in every line of her body.

"You need rest," Soara said. Beneath her usual bluntness, Obi-Wan sensed real concern. He could see why. Curi looked ready to collapse.

Yet somehow Curi reached down and called up a reserve of strength. She straightened and shook her head. "There can be no rest for me. Don't you know that? Not when I'm responsible for this." She looked over the city again. "For all of this horror," she whispered.

"What do you mean?" Siri asked.

"Didn't Galen tell you?" Curi sighed. "We own a research laboratory here. I run the financial side. Galen is the scientist. The toxic emission came from our lab. We still don't understand how it happened, though that doesn't make us any less responsible. Galen has been working day and night on the evacuation effort. He could have left long ago."

"And you?" Obi-Wan asked.

"I was in the Clear Sector, as was Galen, when we heard. I came here. I was trained as a medic originally. Here is where I was most needed."

"It was brave of you to come," Soara said.

Curi pressed her lips together. "It was the least I could do."

"Have you investigated the leak at your lab?" Siri asked.

Curi shook her head. "I didn't have time to review safety procedures, so I just ordered it shut down. It was clear very quickly that we were dealing with something that moved very fast. I came back when I knew we were running out of time to help the sick. We didn't realize that the sick would turn into the dying. We had no idea what to expect. Galen was involved in weapons development, you see. He was experimenting with the toxin for a future bio-weapon. He had no idea what he had."

"What do you know about the toxin?"

"We know more about what it isn't than what it is,"

Curi admitted. "We know it isn't a virus. It isn't a gas, but it has been carried through the air. Somehow it is absorbed into the system, but we aren't sure how. It could be through the skin. The particles are so microscopic that even a bacta bath would not clear it all away."

"It doesn't seem that you have the same problems here that the Clear Sector does," Obi-Wan observed. "There's no sign of panic or rioting."

Curi nodded tiredly. "There was no time for panic. The dying cannot riot. Those who couldn't make it here to the med center are dying in their homes. I make the rounds. I do what I can. That is very little."

"What other kind of help can we give you?" Siri asked.

"You have brought the medicine. That was a great help. Perhaps you could patrol the city and find out how many still need help. I haven't been able to get to every dwelling. You can help us organize. People will listen to you. Once the ships arrive, they will have more advanced med care. We might be able to save a few. You have to give them hope, at least." Curi's voice faltered.

Obi-Wan nodded, then turned to the others. "We should split into two teams. We can call two of the Padawans here, and two Masters can return to the Clear Sector."

Ry-Gaul nodded.

"We might be able to move another team back after we accomplish something here," Soara said as Siri nodded in agreement.

Curi looked from one Jedi to the other. "But you can't return."

"What?" Soara asked.

"Didn't Galen tell you? Once you cross over to the Isolation Sector, no one is allowed to return. It is forbidden. Until we know that you're not carrying the toxin back on your skin or clothes, we can't risk it."

"We're wearing bio-isolation suits," Siri said.

"Yes, but you can't wear them back to the Clear Sector," Curi explained. "The toxin may now be on your suit. Even if you remove it, some residue on the suit may touch your skin. Until we know how much of the toxin is needed to cause the epidemic, we can't let you return." She looked at them helplessly. "I'm sorry. I thought you knew. When the evacuation ships arrive, you will be able to undergo bio-cleansing aboard ship. Then I imagine there will be a quarantine period. We don't have the facilities here."

Obi-Wan looked at the other Jedi Masters. Curi's news was exasperating, but Jedi did not waste time on such emotions. He knew that, like him, they were all thinking of what to do next.

"We should contact our Padawans with more detailed instructions," Soara spoke crisply.

"They will have to handle any problems in Tacto," Siri said. "Perhaps we should contact the Jedi Council and ask for an additional Jedi team, or maybe two."

"By the time they arrive, the evacuation ships will be here," Obi-Wan said. "The Padawans will have to handle things on their own."

He could see that none of them liked this prospect. Some of the Masters had not had their Padawans very long. It made him uneasy to think of Anakin in an unstable situation without him. But there was no other solution.

Obi-Wan activated his comlink. He was relieved when he heard Anakin's voice. He knew the communication between the two sectors could be difficult. That would be another problem.

"We have a problem here," he told Anakin. "We are unable to return to the Clear Sector. You and the rest of the Padawans will have to manage that aspect of the mission."

"I see," Anakin said neutrally.

"The safety of the population is your first priority," Obi-Wan said. "Establish safety patrols to keep the peace. Try to keep misinformation from spreading. Coordinate with Galen as to the evacuation schedule. Avoid using violence, and take no lives."

"Yes, Master."

"Now, as for details," Obi-Wan began, but suddenly, the communication was cut off. When he tried to contact Anakin again, he could not reach him. Obi-wan hid his frustration as he tucked his comlink back in his belt.

"They'll be fine," Siri said. "I trust Ferus. He's been on many missions."

"And I trust Anakin," Obi-Wan agreed. Still, a small voice inside him hoped that Anakin would be able to work well with the other Padawans without his watchful eye.

"We'll try again later," Soara said. "In the meantime, we should split into teams."

Obi-Wan glanced at Siri, and she nodded. There were many times that they had clashed in the past. But that did not matter. They had worked together before and knew each other's rhythms.

"Obi-Wan and I will begin to search the city for more of the sick," Siri said.

"We'll take the north sector," Obi-Wan said. "We need to compile lists so that we can assure there is space for everyone. We must make sure all the sick are evacuated. We'll check in when we can."

Ry-Gaul nodded.

"May the Force be with you," Soara said.

"May the Force be with you," Obi-Wan and Siri repeated. Then they turned toward the eerie emptiness of the city and began their walk toward death.

CHAPTER SEVEN

The Padawans had just left the med center when Obi-Wan contacted Anakin. They had remained to make sure that the Radnoran father would be all right. They had questioned the family, but no one knew the raiders. They had arrived out of nowhere. Other families in the neighborhood had been hit, too, so they'd been worried that they would be attacked. But there was no way to defend themselves against the prototype droids.

The four Padawans paused on the outside of the med center. Suddenly, they felt very alone.

"I spend half my time impatient to be a Jedi Knight," Darra said finally. "Now all I want is to be a Padawan. I wish Soara were here." She reached into the pocket of Tru's tunic and withdrew the bag of candy he kept there.

She popped a piece of figda in her mouth and chewed furiously.

"We'll do fine," Anakin said confidently.

"No stress," Ferus agreed. The expression in his dark eyes was serene. "Among all of us, we've been on enough missions to handle this."

"How should we start?" Tru asked. "Did they want all of us to go on safety patrols? Or should one team coordinate with Galen on the evacuation?"

"Obi-Wan didn't say," Anakin answered. "But if you ask me, safety patrols won't accomplish much if we don't flush out the raiders."

"Hold it," Ferus said. "That would be overstepping our instructions."

"We've received no clear directions," Anakin pointed out. "The communication cut out. We know our first priority is the safety of the citizens, and we can't possibly accomplish that with safety patrols alone."

"You don't know that for sure," Ferus said.

Darra looked from Anakin to Ferus. "Excuse me. I don't want to interrupt, but I just wanted to point out that there are two other Padawans here. Do we get a vote?"

"Sure you get a vote," Anakin said. "As long as you agree with me." He smiled to let her know he was kidding.

"What do you have in mind?" Tru asked Anakin. "Let's discuss the plan first, then vote on it."

"It would be much more fun to stand here arguing," Darra said.

"I say we split into teams," Anakin said. "One team can conduct safety patrols. The other can work on finding the headquarters of the raiders." He knew very well that he wasn't going to be on the team conducting safety patrols. He and Tru would go after the raiders.

"How?" Ferus asked. "We don't have the resources to comb the whole city."

"We don't have to. I have an idea," Anakin declared. "Even a Prototype Droid would have a homing device. All we have to do is take one of the droids we deactivated and tap into it."

"Do you know how to do that?" Darra asked.

"Sure," Anakin replied.

"It can't be that easy," Darra said.

Anakin grinned. "I didn't say it was easy. I said I could do it."

"Hold on a second," Tru said. "These are Battle Droids. Most likely they undergo an automatic memory wipe if they are captured or deactivated."

"There isn't a memory wipe that I can't get around," Anakin said confidently. "The homing device is coded into the main sensor suite. I can find it. If we revive a droid, it will lead us straight to the headquarters."

Darra shrugged. "It's worth a try."

Tru nodded. "All right. I say we go after the head-quarters."

"Then it's decided," Ferus said. "Though I don't think we should split into teams. If Anakin is successful and we do find the headquarters, no doubt there will be more of those Prototype Droids. Too many for one team to handle."

Privately, Anakin thought that he and Tru could han-dle the droids, but he nodded. "All right." Obi-Wan had given him a warning that he must cooperate, respecting Jedi values. Anakin took that seriously.

They headed back to the Radnoran family home. The fallen droids still littered the grounds. Anakin found one that was mostly intact. It had lost its arms and its artillery control panel had fused, but the main sensor suite wasn't too badly damaged.

Anakin removed his utility kit from his belt and went to work. He opened the sensor suite panel. Tru bent over to look.

"Standard, except for those circuits," he said, point-ing. "I remember seeing a manual regarding the OOM-9 Battle Droid. This looks similar."

Anakin was grateful for Tru's photographic memory.

Some of the circuitry was new to him. He pointed to a tightly packed array of multicolored wires by the sensory input cable. "Do you remember which wire goes with what?"

"The green are for locomotion. The white connect to artillery devices. See how they fused and shorted? The blue are for passive-mode sensors. And I think these cables here are part of the signal receiver assembly."

"I bet the homing device is connected somehow," Anakin murmured.

"It's a good place to start," Tru agreed.

Darra seemed interested in their progress, but Anakin could feel Ferus's impatience behind him. He tried to screen it out as he worked.

"I've got it!" Anakin said at last. "I reconnected the homing device to the locomotion sensor through the sensory plug-in. If I turn it on, the droid should head back to its origin point."

"Let's give it a try," Tru said.

"Remind me to get you guys the next time my com-link malfunctions," Darra said. "You'd probably rebuild it into a cargo lifter."

"We'll have to move fast to keep the droid in sight," Ferus said. "Is everyone ready?"

When he saw everyone nod, Anakin switched on the droid. They stepped back as it beeped and checked circuits. Then suddenly it wheeled around and fired its repulsorlift engines, taking off down the boulevard.

The four Padawans had to race to keep it in sight. They flew down the streets of the city, occasionally Force-jumping past obstacles. They quickly passed through the neighborhood of fine homes, raced through a commercial district, and then found themselves outside a small warehouse. The droid hovered outside for a moment, its head rotating. The Padawans dived behind a wall.

They watched as the droid accessed a control panel hidden behind what appeared to be a sheer wall. A door slid open, and the droid disappeared inside.

Anakin leaped forward and shoved his lightsaber hilt between the closing door and its frame. The door stayed open a fraction. With Tru, Ferus, and Darra, he pushed it open the rest of the way. The Padawans slid inside.

It was a gloomy interior. At first they could see or hear little. Anakin concentrated. He detected the sound of voices. He motioned to the others. When their eyes had adjusted to the light a few moments later, they could see that the warehouse was full of items they could only assume were stolen. Rich tapestries and rugs were rolled and rested against the walls. Silver and intricate metalwork objects were stacked on shelves. Anakin saw gold peggats and aurodium ingots heaped in a corner. Durasteel bins were no doubt filled with more valuables.

The voices were coming from around the corner. It was the raiders.

The Padawans crept closer. Now they could make out words.

"The bloc between Evermore and Acadi is first. Then from Acadi to Montwin. We can easily clear out the two blocs using what we have."

"Sure we can clear them, but where will we put our stash? We need more storage."

"That's one problem I'm happy to have."

The sound of soft laughter came to the Padawans.

"They'd better come through on their promise to move all this stuff —"

The voice broke off as an insistent beep began to sound. It played through several coded sequences.

Anakin heard the sound of chairs scraping. "It's the droid," someone said in a low tone. "That's the activation signal for tampering. Someone might be here." The voices fell silent. Anakin could just make out a whisper of movement, and then stillness.

"Activation signal for tampering?" Darra whispered.

Anakin and Tru exchanged a look. "I guess it's in case the homing device is activated by someone other than the programmer," Anakin explained.

"*Easy,* you said," Darra whispered. "What should we do now?"

"Defend ourselves!" Anakin exclaimed as the raiders suddenly raced around the corner, blasters in hand.

CHAPTER EIGHT

They had been ordered to take no lives. Somehow they would have to deflect blaster fire and capture the raiders without harming them.

As Anakin swung his lightsaber in a blur, deflecting fire, he realized for the first time that they had overlooked something.

If they caught the raiders, what would they do with them?

There weren't enough security officers to guard the criminals. The Jedi were now the backbone of the security force on the planet. If they watched the raiders, who would patrol the city?

The present moment is the crucial moment.

Yes, Master. Anakin gritted his teeth. He advanced toward the raiders. One thing at a time. The raiders were endangering the citizens and must be stopped. The Padawans would figure out what to do with them when the time came.

One of the raiders must have activated some droids, for suddenly they appeared. They wheeled into battle formation and came at the Padawans.

Anakin at first felt confident that he could defeat the droids. He had not fully realized how much he had depended earlier on the Jedi Masters. Within moments he saw that they would have a hard time winning this battle.

He hated to admit it. Ferus had been right. He and Tru could not have handled these droids by themselves.

The raiders maneuvered the droids to come between them and the Jedi. Then they disappeared. Too occupied with the attacking droids, the Padawans could not follow.

"We've got to stay together!" Ferus shouted. "Don't let them separate us."

Ferus was right again. As one unit, they could defeat fifteen droids. The Padawans kept close together, attacking and retreating, trying to pick up on one another's unfamiliar rhythms. Anakin lost himself in the battle. There was only the smell of the smoking droids, the blur of his lightsaber, the balance and heft of it in his hand. He saw everything at once — the position of each Padawan, the attack pattern of each droid, the moves they would make next. His focus was complete. He sliced through one droid, then pivoted and buried his lightsaber in another droid's control panel.

Ferus dived and came up underneath a droid, halving it down the middle. Tru whirled and kicked one droid while cutting off the legs of another. Darra seemed to be everywhere, her lightsaber in constant motion as she took out one droid, then another. She always landed exactly where she'd planned, ready to launch another attack or defend her fellow Padawans. Her face never registered effort, only concentration. She had learned well from Soara Antana.

At last the droids lay in heaps around them. The Padawans all slumped to the floor, exhausted. They missed their Masters.

"We still might be able to track the raiders," Anakin said, panting. He started to rise. "Let's go."

"Wait." Ferus put a hand on his sleeve. "If we run off, we could lose a precious opportunity."

"For what, droid repair?" Anakin asked.

"Information. It's more important than the raiders themselves. What will we do with them when we get them, anyway?" Ferus asked. "Better to head them off another way. We have more important tasks. Once the evacuation starts, we'll be needed."

"That could be a waste of time," Anakin argued. "We could catch the raiders if we follow them now. I want to show Obi-Wan that I can handle a complicated mission."

"You mean you want to help the planet," Ferus said pointedly.

Anakin felt his face grow hot. Of course Ferus was right. Ferus gave the correct Jedi response. Anakin's first concern should be the people of Radnor, not his need to impress Obi-Wan. He had just expressed himself badly. He had blurted out what was in the back of his mind, not what was in the front of it. He wished he wouldn't keep running into the fact that Ferus took a more Jedi approach to action.

"What are you thinking, Ferus?" Darra asked curiously.

"We need to examine this hideout," Ferus said. "I have a feeling it has something to teach us."

"What can it teach us?" Anakin asked. "That the raiders like riches?"

Darra ignored Anakin. "Remember what we heard? Evermore and Acadi and Montwin are probably street names. They're not just striking randomly. They have a plan."

Ferus nodded. "If we can figure out their plan, we can be ahead of them instead of behind them."

"There's got to be a datapad here somewhere," Tru said, rising. "They left too fast to destroy their records."

Anakin trailed after the others. His whole body itched to follow the raiders. He always felt more comfortable in physical activity. He always ached to move. But he hoped he was wise enough to realize when it was better to wait. He just wasn't crazy about the fact that Ferus was the one to suggest it.

He knew what Obi-Wan would say. It didn't matter who suggested it. The outcome was the goal. Resentment was ego. He knew all this, but it did not chase the resentment away.

You can feel the emotion, Obi-Wan would say. *Just let it go.*

Anakin gritted his teeth. *I'm trying, Master.*

"Over here!" Darra called. "I found their holofiles."

The files had been concealed in a durasteel bin just like countless others that lined the walls.

"How did you find them?" Anakin asked.

Darra was already accessing the files. "I figured that they had been consulting the files while they were talking. The slight delay before they came to attack us meant they were concealing them. They had to be nearby."

"Good thinking," Tru said admiringly.

The Padawans bent over the files. Darra expertly accessed one after the other.

"These are lists of assets held by individual families," Anakin said. "How could they have gotten them?"

"Look at these notations," Tru said. "They're coded ECC."

"Emergency Command Center," Darra murmured.

"These files were drawn up so that if the entire planet had to be evacuated, there would be records of what Radnorans left behind," Tru said. "That way they could recover everything later."

"So the raiders must have stolen these files," Ferus added.

"Or bribed someone on the evacuation team to hand them over," Darra said. "Look at this. This is what they were talking about. They have a list of how the evacuation is going to take place. The first group to be evacuated will be from the bloc between Evermore and Acadi. As soon as those families evacuate, the raiders will move in and clean them out."

Tru gave a low whistle. "That's some organized system. But why are they looting now?"

"Easy answer?" Darra shrugged. "Because they can."

Anakin nodded. "The city is falling apart, and they see an opportunity. But are they counting on coming back to the planet for this stuff, or do they have plans to take it with them? It would be hard to smuggle it aboard the evacuation ship. The families are only allowed what they can carry."

Tru reached around his head with one flexible arm to scratch his ear thoughtfully. "The raiders said something about 'they' had better come through on their promise to move the stuff. Who's 'they'?"

"Maybe they have a contact who will help them smuggle it," Ferus said, frowning.

Darra looked up at them, her face tinged blue by the light cast by the holofile. "The important thing is that they have access to all the evacuation orders. That means someone on the inside is helping them."

"Well, at least we know exactly what to do next," Anakin said. "We have to find out who."

He looked over at Ferus. He expected his fellow Padawan to argue, but Ferus nodded.

"And *why*," Ferus added. "That might be the most important question of all."

CHAPTER NINE

It wasn't hard work, Obi-Wan told himself. It was just heartbreaking.

He and Siri moved through a landscape that reminded him of a desert moon. Yes, there were buildings. Homes. Businesses. Shops. But the eerie absence of lives being lived made the city a vast echo of sorrow.

They found the dead and they found the still-living. They brought the sick to the overcrowded med center, where medication only slowed the process of dying. Curi had had hopes that the medication could effect some cures, but so far it had not. The toxin did not respond.

Every so often Obi-Wan and Siri would see Ry-Gaul and Soara on their rounds. The four Jedi would simply nod at one another. There was nothing to say. No notes to compare. There was only death and the dying.

On their last trip to the med center, Siri watched as Obi-Wan deactivated his comlink after another unsuccessful effort to contact Anakin. "You seem worried," she said.

Obi-Wan thought carefully how to reply. He didn't want Siri to think he didn't trust Anakin. How could she understand? Her Padawan was Ferus, who Obi-Wan knew as an assured, steady Jedi student. No one understood his brilliant, openhearted, complex Padawan like he did.

So yes, I'm worried, Obi-Wan thought. *But I will only admit that to myself. I don't worry that Anakin will fail. Or that he will let down the Order. But that he will try too hard. That he will go too far. That he will assume he can do what he cannot.*

"I'd rather he was by my side," he said. "That's all."

Siri nodded, her clear blue eyes holding a hint of skepticism. She knew he was not telling her the complete truth. Obi-Wan turned away. Sometimes old friends were hard to have around.

Suddenly, Curi hailed them from the steps of the med center. Her eyes were red-rimmed behind her bio-iso mask.

"The ambassador from Avon wishes to speak with you," she said. "His name is Dol Heep. He was trapped here when he entered shortly before the toxin release. He wore a bio-iso suit so hasn't been affected, but he can't leave. He has a proposal."

"Avon is a planet in your system," Obi-Wan said. He remembered that the planet was only a day's journey away.

Curi nodded. "He is waiting for you. You can use my office."

They followed Curi's directions to a small, cluttered office. Sleep mats were rolled up and stacked in the corners. Containers of food were scattered on a long table. Obviously the medics used the office to snatch quick meals and some rest when they could.

Dol Heep rose when they entered. He was a tall being with a large, domed head. He was dressed in a bio-iso suit, though for some reason he had attached his ornate septsilk cloak to it, which gave him a slightly ridiculous air.

He bowed. "A great honor to meet Jedi." His voice boomed out, sounding too loud in the hushed setting.

Siri and Obi-Wan returned the bow.

"Unfortunate that it is under such circumstances," Dol Heep continued. "No one in the government is available for us to speak with. Jedi are the only officials we can approach with this offer."

"Yes?" Siri asked, inclining her head politely.

"Avon grieves at the tragic accident that has befallen our neighbor," Dol Heep said in a slightly lowered tone, his prominent eyes staring at them from behind his mask. "We heard that there might not be enough room on the evacuation ships for everyone here."

"That is a rumor," Obi-Wan said. "It is false."

"So you say. In case of some failure, Avon wishes to send an entire fleet to Radnor to airlift more sick off-planet. We took the liberty of sending the fleet already. Once in orbit, we'll await orders. Of course, we'll need Jedi help here on the ground to coordinate the rescue effort."

"That is a kind and generous offer," Obi-Wan said. "But there is no need for Avon to commit a fleet of vessels. There is enough space on the ships being sent by the Senate."

"This information does not seem to have been accepted by the citizens of Radnor," Dol Heep said. "Appearance is often reality. If more ships are said to be arriving, the people will be more calm."

Dol Heep had a point. Even the rumor of another rescue fleet could calm the population. But Obi-Wan felt uneasy. He wasn't about to accept the offer until he knew more. He gave a quick glance to Siri. He could see the same doubt in her eyes.

"We will get back to you," he said.

"My planet appreciates your consideration," Dol Heep said. With another bow, he left the room.

Obi-Wan turned to Siri. "What do you think?"

"There's something about this that isn't right," Siri said. "I just have a feeling about it." Her blue eyes gleamed at him in a way he hadn't seen since they'd arrived on Radnor. There hadn't been much call for Siri's quick wit. "I trust my instincts, but you know how I occasionally like to back them up with facts."

"Until we have facts, let's hold off, then," Obi-Wan agreed. "We should investigate the offer further."

Curi poked her head in the room. "Are you finished? I have some medics who need to eat or they'll collapse."

"Tell them to come in," Siri said. "What do you know about Dol Heep, Curi?"

Curi tried to scratch her scalp through her bio-iso suit. "Not much. But what I know I don't trust. Radnorans don't trust the Avoni. They are aggressive colonizers. I made it a rule not to do business with them. I wouldn't sell them weapons. Of course, there are many others, even on Radnor, who will." Her face changed. "There *were* many others," she added softly.

"Avon has offered a fleet of evacuation ships for

Radnor," Obi-Wan told her. "I don't feel we should take the offer at face value."

Curi looked puzzled. "What are you getting at?"

"For one thing, the offer could be a smokescreen for a planned takeover," Siri said.

Curi frowned. "Why would Avon want to take over a planet where you can't breathe the air?"

"A good point," Obi-Wan said. "Maybe Avon doesn't want to colonize Radnor. But they might be planning a temporary occupation. There are many tech labs on Radnor that can be plundered for data. Sometimes data can be more important than land."

Curi just looked tired. "I can't worry about this. I have sick people to take care of."

Siri put a gloved hand on her shoulder. "We will handle it."

Curi nodded and left. Obi-Wan and Siri headed out of the med center. He hoped it would not be a waste of time to investigate the Avoni.

The offer seemed a simple offer of help from a neighbor. But he had been on enough missions to know that there were veils behind veils, where somewhere the truth would lie.

CHAPTER TEN

The Padawans were heading into the Emergency Command Center when Ferus held up a hand. The Padawans stopped. Anakin nearly bumped into Darra. Annoyed, he stepped back.

"Before we meet with Galen, I suggest that only one Padawan conduct the questioning," Ferus said. "We don't want him to think we are accusing or bullying him. This should be done carefully."

"You should do it, Ferus," Darra said. "You have the most experience."

Ferus nodded. "All right."

Wait a second. Don't I get a vote? Anakin wondered. What happened to Jedi cooperation?

But Tru was agreeing as well, so Anakin nodded.

Ferus led the way into the room, which had been a

minister's office before all the government officials had fled the planet. Now a row of datascreens glowed faintly as Galen sat on a repulsorlift chair, moving from screen to screen as he checked and matched lists.

"How is the evacuation coming?" Ferus asked politely as they entered.

Galen passed a harried hand through his hair. "All right. There are so many details. And I don't have much help."

"We'd be glad to assist you," Ferus said. "How many workers do you have here?"

"Just me at the moment," Galen said. "I had a staff, but they all left when the ministers did." He gave the Padawans an impatient glance. "I can handle things here. You go ahead and keep patrolling the streets, or whatever you're doing." He turned back to the datascreens, dismissing the Padawans as though they were naughty children who had interrupted his work.

"Can you tell us who has access to this information?" Ferus asked. Anakin was surprised at his polite tone. How could he let Galen get away with patronizing them?

"The upper ministers of government had access," Galen answered without turning. "And now I do. Why?"

"Is there anyone who would release that information?" Ferus asked.

Galen gave a weary sigh and turned around in his chair. "No, of course not," he said. "It's classified. Sensitive. If people knew in what order they would be evacuating, violence could erupt. The people at the bottom of the list will try to push themselves forward. I won't post the lists until immediately before the ships arrive." Galen looked at the Jedi curiously. "If there is something wrong, you must tell me. I am in charge of the city's security. I don't want the job, but I'm the only qualified one left."

"I'm afraid we have reason to believe that the raiders have information about the evacuation," Ferus answered. "We believe they are planning to plunder the homes of those who are leaving the planet."

Galen looked at them sharply. "Are you sure about this?" At Ferus's nod, he shook his head. "Still, at least they will have their lives."

"But they will return to nothing," Darra said.

"If we *can* return." Galen looked away. "I have a feeling our beloved planet is lost to us for good."

"You don't know that," Ferus said. "The toxin could have a half-life."

"We don't have time to investigate that," Galen snapped. "Don't you think we have enough to do?"

"We are not accusing you," Ferus said politely.

"Maybe not. But you are wasting my time. I am try-ing to save lives here." Galen waved at the datascreen.

"We need to find out who passed the information along," Anakin said in a forceful tone. He was tired of letting Ferus ask all the questions. He was getting nowhere with that polite tone. "Whoever it was wanted to foster instability on the planet. I don't call investigat-ing that a waste of time. Do you?"

"Hey, there's no reason to jump down my throat, kid." Galen held up two hands, as if to fend Anakin off. "Look, I'd like to help. But there's really no way to tell who passed on the information. Many of the ministers have gone to Coruscant. Some have scattered to other worlds to wait out the catastrophe in comfort." He frowned at them. "You're not thinking of leaving now that you've lost your Masters, are you?"

"We haven't lost them," Anakin snapped.

Ferus interrupted smoothly. "No, we're not leaving. We're to remain until the evacuations take place. Don't worry. And we've destroyed many of the Prototype Droids that the raiders were using."

"You kids did?" Galen looked impressed. "Maybe things are looking up." Suddenly the communicator sputtered to life. It crackled and buzzed, but they could hear a voice calling for Galen to answer.

He quickly adjusted the chair to swing over to the comm unit. "Galen here. Galen here. Do you read? Do you read?"

"Ships . . . evacuation . . . engine shutdown needs repair . . ." The words came out in bursts of static. "Delay. Do you copy?"

"The ships are delayed? How long?" Galen asked desperately. "How long?"

But the comm unit went dead.

Galen turned to the Padawans. His face was pale. "That was the communication line of the Senate ship. Even a short delay will be fatal. The winds will shift in twelve hours. Without those ships, we're dead."

CHAPTER ELEVEN

In the Isolation Sector, the Jedi Masters met outside the med center to check in. Soara and Ry-Gaul
were also hesitant about Dol Heep's offer.

"The planet is extremely vulnerable now," Soara
said. "One day the survivors will want to return, if they
can. They should return to intact homes and businesses."

"This will take further study," Siri said soberly.

Ry-Gaul nodded.

Just then Curi hurried out of the building. "I've received a communication from the evacuation ships. It
wasn't very clear, but I do know this — the ships have
been delayed. How long, I don't know."

The Jedi exchanged glances. Obi-Wan reached for
his comlink and tried to contact Anakin. He was unsuc-

cessful. He jammed it back into his belt with unneces-sary force. Siri glanced at him, then turned back to the others.

"Now we must take Dol Heep's offer seriously," Siri said worriedly. "Lives are at stake."

"The prevailing winds will shift in twelve hours," Obi-Wan said. "We have to make a decision very soon."

"By the way, we encountered something interest-ing," Soara said. "We found someone who has been unaffected by the toxin."

Curi's worried expression changed to intent curios-ity. "What do you mean?"

"A Radnoran named Wilk sneaked back into the Iso-lation Sector to see his wife two days ago. He didn't have a bio-iso suit. His wife died, but he is completely healthy."

"He has no symptoms at all?" Curi asked. "Are you sure?"

"We brought him here," Soara told her. "We were just about to look for you."

"We must study him," Curi said, her voice rising with excitement. "He could have some sort of built-in immu-nity. This could help us." She frowned. "I only have a few researchers here. My scientific skills are rusty, but we need to investigate this."

"There isn't much time," Obi-Wan told her.

For the first time since they'd met her, Curi smiled. "Then I'd better get started."

She turned and rushed back into the building.

A voice suddenly boomed out from behind them. "Jedi! Glad to find you here."

It was Dol Heep. The Jedi bowed to him politely.

"You haven't been back to speak to us as you promised," Dol Heep said. "We don't understand this lack of courtesy."

"We have been busy with the sick," Siri said.

"You should be busy working to get them off-planet," Dol Heep said in a chiding tone. "Our planet has made a great and generous offer, and still you ignore us. Now we hear that the evacuation ships have been delayed. And you *still* don't come to us?" Dol Heep's skin was mottled with anger. "We deserve this treatment? If you do not allow our fleet to land, the Senate shall hear about it!"

"We were just coming to see you, Dol Heep," Obi-Wan said in a polite tone, even though he was nettled at the ambassador's rudeness. "We accept your offer of help."

It was a decision he'd made reluctantly. But Siri was right. Lives were at stake. The Jedi would just have to ensure that the Avoni were not planning a takeover of the famed Radnoran research labs. Though how they would do that, he didn't know. The Senate ships could be delayed for days. It was more than time enough for the Avoni to raid the labs.

"More like it, we say," Dol Heep said, satisfied. "We will give the order for the ferry ships to land in both sectors. We will load the citizens onto skiffs in the cities, then bring them to the ferry ships, which will transport them to the orbiting ships. Then we'll bring them to Coruscant. You see? We give all our resources to our friends the Radnorans."

Dol Heep hurried off, his septsilk cloak swishing with his lurching walk.

"I hope we don't come to regret this," Soara said.

"Yes," Obi-Wan said. "But it seems the only decision to make under the circumstances."

Siri withdrew her comlink from her utility belt. She punched out the coordinates for Ferus. To everyone's surprise, they heard Ferus's voice clearly.

"Yes, Master."

"Ferus! We have received word that the evacuation ships have been delayed —"

"We know this. And Master —"

"One minute, Ferus," Siri interrupted. "This is important. Avoni ships will be here in a matter of hours. They will transport the population to ships orbiting the planet. Then they'll be taken to safety. There is no need for panic. Did you copy that?"

"Yes, Master. But we fear that someone has —"

Static overcame the line, and it went dead.

The Masters exchanged uneasy glances.

"He sounded worried," Obi-Wan said.

"Yes," Siri agreed quietly. "He did."

"Something is wrong in Tacto," Soara murmured. "I can feel it. But I don't have a clear sense of it."

The Jedi Masters exchanged glances. They all felt the same.

"I agree," Siri said. "We can only trust that our Padawans are able to handle it."

The usually composed Soara looked uncertain. "This is Darra's first mission."

"Ferus has experience with difficult situations," Siri said. "And the others look up to him."

Not Anakin, Obi-Wan thought. He had sensed Anakin's dislike of Ferus. It hadn't worried him. Anakin would naturally feel rivalries with other Padawans at this age. As he matured as a Jedi, he would outgrow them. Once, Obi-Wan had felt the same about Siri. Now he valued her friendship.

Anakin was still young. Without Obi-Wan there to guide him, would Anakin allow his strong will to bend with the needs of the group? Would his dislike of Ferus spill over into open conflict? The nagging doubts would not go away.

"They are all excellent Padawans, each in their own way," Soara said confidently. "Together they are even stronger."

"But they are not Jedi," Ry-Gaul said softly. "Not yet."

And somehow these gentle words from a Jedi who rarely spoke summed up everything they felt. And everything they feared.

CHAPTER TWELVE

Ferus was right. Ferus was always right. Except when he was wrong.

Anakin hurried along the streets of Tacto with the others. News of the delay of the evacuation ships had leaked out. Security officers had called for help. A riot had broken out in the last remaining shop to sell bio-isolation suits. While he raced along with the others, Anakin's mind was busy furiously reviewing the scene with Galen. Ferus's too-respectful questioning had gotten them nowhere. As soon as Anakin began to make some headway, Ferus had interrupted.

"You handled Galen well back there," Darra said to Ferus. "I don't think I could have held my temper."

"It does us no good to make him angry," Ferus said. "He is still a source of information for us."

Anakin snorted. "Some source. He didn't tell us anything. He treated us like kids. And you let him get away with it."

Ferus glanced down and gave him a cool look as he kept up his easy, loping stride. Anakin wished he weren't so tall. "He didn't tell you anything, either."

"He was about to," Anakin shot back.

"So you can see into the future," Ferus said. "Hmmm. That's very unusual for a Padawan."

Anakin flushed angrily as Darra giggled.

"As long as we keep our lightsabers sheathed," Tru spoke up suddenly. The three Padawans looked at him. "We can handle the riot peacefully," he explained.

Now they could hear the roar of the crowd ahead. They picked up their pace and raced to the spot.

Blasters had been drawn. Radnorans lay bleeding on the streets. More pushed to get inside the store. Bio-iso suits had been torn to shreds by competing Radnorans. Over a voice amp system, the shop owner was desperately attempting to quiet the crowd.

"There are no more suits!" he cried. "No more suits! Go home! The shop is empty!"

"We need to get to the voice amp," Anakin said.

"Keep your lightsabers sheathed," Ferus warned. "We can handle this peacefully if we keep calm."

Ferus was giving orders again. Anakin turned away

and tried to push his way through the crowd. Darra and Tru joined Ferus in breaking up fights and trying to calm the crowd. It was difficult to do this without hurting anyone. At first the Radnorans were furious at the Jedi. They had to dodge blows as they sought to calm tempers.

Anakin made his way to the frightened owner. "I must use your voice amp," he told him. "I can calm the crowd."

The owner handed him the amp. "Be my guest."

Anakin spoke clearly into the amp system. "The Avoni have pledged a fleet of ships to airlift the citizens off-planet. They are achieving orbit now. There is room for all. Everyone will be evacuated before the winds shift."

A few Radnorans closest to the amp heard the message and began to talk among themselves. Anakin repeated the message. Gradually, the crowd began to settle down.

"Where do we report to? How will this be handled?" someone called.

"The evacuation team will alert each of you where and when to show up," Anakin announced. "But that means you must return to your homes."

Slowly the crowd began to disperse. The crisis was averted. But the owner's business had been completely destroyed. The battered sign reading BIO-ISO SUITS 5,000 KARSEMS swung crazily in the stiff breeze.

"It almost serves him right for charging so much," Darra said as a last burst of wind sent the sign crashing to the street.

"I wish communication were better with our Masters," Tru said. "They will know when and how the Avoni fleet is arriving. We need to give the Radnorans more information."

"I think we should take a look at the comm system," Anakin said. "There might be a way to fix it, or at least fabricate a makeshift comm unit that has enough power to reach the other sector."

Ferus shook his head. "We won't be able to fix a planetary system," he said. "Atmospheric disturbances are too great."

"We don't know that," Anakin argued. "It's worth a try. We need to coordinate with the other sector."

"Here we go again," Darra said, looking from Anakin to Ferus. "Don't you two ever agree?"

Anakin looked at Tru. He needed backup.

"I think we should try it," Tru said.

"Why not?" Darra agreed. "We're at a dead end, anyway."

Ferus nodded. "All right. But while you and Tru work

on the comm problem, Darra and I should investigate those Prototype Droids. Maybe if we find out how they were stolen, we can find out more about the raiders. I'm still worried about who is behind them."

So am I, Anakin said silently. *We all are.*

The two Padawan teams split up. Anakin and Tru retraced their steps back to the Emergency Command Center. They needed to get permission from Galen to access the central power source.

"Why not?" Galen said, waving a hand. "Our tech experts can't fix it. Give it a try."

Anakin and Tru entered the comm center. "Thanks for backing me up," Anakin said. "Have you noticed how Ferus has been taking control?"

"No," Tru said. "I've noticed he's had some good ideas. So have you."

"Well, I don't like being bossed around," Anakin muttered.

Tru gave him a sidelong look. "This isn't a game of sabaac, Anakin. No one is keeping score. We're all just trying to do the right thing."

"I don't like the way he operates, that's all," Anakin said.

Tru shook his head. "You're doing the same thing he's doing, Anakin. You're thinking ahead. You're coming up with ideas. You two are the most experienced

Padawans on the mission. It's natural. I like Ferus. You would, too, if you gave him a chance. He has plenty of friends for a reason."

"Ferus doesn't have friends. He has followers," Anakin said. He didn't like the way the conversation was going, so he began to study the console. "This is pretty standard."

Tru bent over some large-scale holofiles. "I found the blueprint of the system," he said. "We should be able to pinpoint the problem. Fixing it is another matter."

"Let me try the rangefinders first," Anakin said. He bent over the tech console, his fingers flying. He was lucky that he had excelled in his tech classes. He hadn't been content to merely learn what the Masters had wanted him to. He had haunted the tech rooms at the Temple, eager to find out how everything worked.

Anakin tried sending a series of messages, then backtracked through the system, attempting to locate the precise problem.

Puzzled, Anakin frowned.

"I know, I don't get it, either," Tru said, jumping into the middle of a conversation they weren't having, as he usually did. "It doesn't make sense. If the toxin had created a disturbance in the atmosphere, the sensors should be recording the activity."

"Everything checks out on the planet itself," Anakin said, clicking a few more keys. "The system should be working."

"Only it isn't," Tru said. "You've got to trust reality over a sensor. No matter how much it hurts."

"Sensors don't lie unless they're broken," Anakin said. "And these aren't." Suddenly, he looked up and met Tru's silvery gaze.

"No," Tru said.

"Yes," Anakin said. "What else can it be? The comm system isn't being jammed in the planetary atmosphere. It's being jammed from space."

Tru whistled under his breath. "Which means someone, somewhere, wants to cut the planet off. And that can only mean one thing."

"Invasion," they said together.

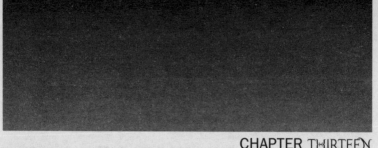

CHAPTER THIRTEEN

Curi sat in the office, a plate of untouched food pushed away from her and a datapad in front of her. She rested her head against her hand, and, behind her mask, her eyes were closed.

Obi-Wan and Siri paused. If Curi was resting at last, they didn't want to disturb her.

Without opening her eyes, she spoke. "We can't find it. Whatever makes Wilk immune to the toxin, we might never know. We've checked out everything."

"I'm sorry," Siri said.

Curi opened her eyes. She started to scratch her head, then remembered she was in her bio-iso suit. She grimaced. "There's something else. We used our lab facilities to run the tests. While we waited for results, I looked up everything on the toxin. I'd already done that when this first happened, but things were moving so fast . . . I didn't have time to look closely. There are gaps in the research."

"What do you mean?" Obi-Wan asked. "Gaps in the way it was conducted?"

"No," Curi said. "Gaps in the records. There are files missing."

"So it's possible that —" Siri began.

"That the accident wasn't an accident," Curi finished.

They left Curi, who was about to return to her lab to investigate further. Obi-Wan looked at Siri.

"The ferry ships should have landed by now."

She nodded. "Let's go."

The Avoni fleet had landed on the outskirts of the Isolation Sector. Obi-Wan and Siri took Curi's air-speeder, which she'd made available for their use. They stopped the speeder a few hundred meters away from the ferry ships, hiding it behind a rocky outcropping.

The wind was strong here, driving the dust against their clothes. The bio-iso suits protected their eyes and skin from the peppery blasts.

The gleaming black ships had landed in formation. A few Avoni workers dressed in bio-iso suits were ferrying skiffs out the cargo loading doors.

"No doubt they're going to use the skiffs to ferry the Radnorans from Aubendo to the fleet," Obi-Wan murmured. "There must be another ship on the other side of the energy gate for Tacto."

"Then why off-load them now?" Siri asked. "And why are they full of durasteel crates?"

"Good question," Obi-Wan said. "Let's get closer."

They moved from rock to rock, trying to get close enough to see what was inside the skiffs. As they lingered in the shadow of a ship's wing, the passenger ramp suddenly lowered. An Avoni officer strode down.

"Progress report!" he called out to the workers.

The worker quickly approached him with a datapad. Obi-Wan glanced at Siri, and after a wordless communication they both dashed up the passenger ramp.

The ship hallway was deserted. Quickly they made their way down it. Now they were in the cargo hold of the ship. There were no ground craft here. No guards or officers.

Obi-Wan accessed a door, keeping himself well out of sight as it slid open. He peered into the doorway. He found himself looking inside a large cargo bay. It was filled with Battle Droids that were ominously familiar.

"These are the Prototype Droids we fought in the Clear Sector," Siri said. "How did the Avoni get them?"

They stepped through the doorway. At that instant, a detector light turned red.

"Mistake," Obi-Wan muttered. "I think we just tripped a silent sensor."

Suddenly an alarm sounded. "Intruder," a pleasant voice announced. "Intruder."

"Not so silent," Siri said grimly. "Let's get out of here while we can."

But even as they turned, the first line of attack droids snapped to life. Behind them, the next line flipped into position. And blaster fire erupted around the Jedi.

CHAPTER FOURTEEN

Obi-Wan and Siri knew that they were no match for this many droids. And at any moment, Avoni troops could appear. Blaster fire pinged around them. Behind them, the door began to slide shut.

Obi-Wan and Siri deflected blaster fire as they moved backward. The frequency of the fire was astonishing. The air filled with smoke. In their bio-iso suits, the Jedi could not move with their customary grace. Obi-Wan felt blaster fire uncomfortably close to his shoulder.

"Obi-Wan!" Siri called.

The doors were closing, and they were too far to make it.

Obi-Wan stepped forward and, with one smooth motion, sliced a droid in half. He took the severed trunk of the body and tossed it back just in time to land between the closing door and the wall. With a grating noise, the door closed on the droid. The metal began to compress with a terrible groaning sound as the door struggled to shut. The gap was just wide enough for Siri to fit through. Even as she squeezed past, the door was closing. Obi-Wan's lightsaber danced, a blade of light that deflected the ongoing blaster fire of the droids. He squeezed through the opening after Siri. A Prototype Droid tried to follow and smashed into the door. Obi-Wan tumbled into the hallway as another droid fired between the gap. Blaster fire zinged past their ears. The droid tried to barrel its way through the remains of the first droid and the closing door.

Obi-Wan and Siri didn't hesitate. As more droids thudded against the half-closed door, they ran for the ramp.

The Avoni officer was still busy with the workers. He must have received a shipboard communication through his headset, for he turned and scanned the area. "Intruders!" he snapped to the workers. "Leave the skiffs. Secure the ferry ships! Lock down all cargo holds!"

The workers began to move. In their bio-iso suits, Obi-Wan and Siri were able to blend in. They made their way along the line of ships, looking busy. Then they ducked behind the rocks and doubled back to their speeder.

They jumped inside and took off.

"At least we weren't seen," Obi-Wan said. "The Avoni won't know we're on to them."

"They'll know someone was aboard when they find several smashed droids and a broken door," Siri said as she piloted the speeder.

"They could think that it was a droid malfunction," Obi-Wan said. "At least for a while."

"Well, that reminds me. What exactly *are* we on to?" Siri asked. "If all of those cargo holds are full of Battle Droids, we're in trouble. What I don't understand is how they're going to get the droids to Aubendo. It seems like they're using the skiffs for cargo."

"I don't know. But there's no doubt in my mind that the Avoni are planning an invasion," Obi-Wan said. "That much is clear. But we have a worse problem."

Siri nodded, her clear blue eyes suddenly clouded. "We might have to let them."

They found Ry-Gaul and Soara with Curi. Ry-Gaul and Soara were studying some results on Curi's datapad. Everyone looked grave.

"Bad news?" Siri asked.

"No, it's actually good news," Curi said. "It's just

puzzling news. We discovered why Wilk is immune to the toxin. He was never exposed at all."

"What do you mean?" Obi-Wan asked. "He sneaked back into the Isolation Sector."

"Exactly. And he didn't get infected," Curi said. "When none of the immunity tests checked out, I went back and checked the research. We ran more tests. The toxin has a short half-life. The poison is already benign. It doesn't threaten the Clear Sector at all."

"Are you absolutely certain of this?" Siri asked.

For her answer, Curi slowly removed her mask. Then she stepped out of her bio-isolation suit.

"I am willing to test it," she said. "I suggest you keep your suits on, for now. If I'm wrong, you should be here to run things."

Obi-Wan admired Curi's courage. "If you're right, this is good news," Obi-Wan said. "We suspect that Avon is attempting a takeover of your planet."

"Wait a second," Siri said. "They *must* know the toxin has dispersed. That's the key to their takeover. They get everyone off-planet, and then they move in."

"But the Avoni were wearing bio-iso suits," Obi-Wan said.

Siri shrugged. "Just in case someone came by — like we did."

"Maybe that accounts for the missing research

records," Soara said. "Could someone have gotten past your security system, Curi?"

Curi didn't say anything for a moment.

"Curi, we don't have time for your hesitations," Soara prodded bluntly.

"No, our security is first-rate," Curi said hesitantly.

"So it would have to be an inside job," Obi-Wan said.

Curi bit her lip. "I want to say no. But there is something I haven't told you about Dol Heep. I've had direct dealings with him. Somehow he found out we were working to develop a new weapon with that toxin. The Avoni wanted exclusive rights to it. They were willing to pay a fortune. I was opposed — I have told you of my feelings about the Avoni. Not to mention that we weren't even close to completion of our research. But Galen wanted to do the deal. He pointed out that we sell to anyone in the galaxy who will pay the price. Why stop now? He had a point. He did not like that I had come to believe we needed to do business a different way. We had terrible arguments. In the end we agreed that our relationship as brother and sister was more important than business. So Galen agreed to my point of view. He had no choice, really. He wouldn't be able to run the lab. He's strictly a research scientist. Dol Heep was furious at our refusal to deal with his planet. When the toxin was released, I just assumed it was an accident."

"And now?" Soara prodded when Curi fell silent.

"And now I'm wondering why Galen didn't know that the toxin has a short half-life," Curi burst out. "He was the one who developed it. How could Galen have made this mistake? How could he not have known?"

"I think you know the answer to that," Obi-Wan said. "He does know."

CHAPTER FIFTEEN

When Ferus and Darra arrived at the communication center, they were shocked at the news that the communications were being jammed from space.

Darra grabbed the end of her sandy Padawan braid and chewed on it nervously. "Do you think it's the Avoni?"

Anakin and Ferus nodded at the same time.

"It sure looks that way," Ferus said. He glanced at the communication console, then at Anakin and Tru. "Good work, you two. I never could have figured out that system."

"It's a perfect plan," Tru said. "Evacuate everyone off-planet. They all go willingly. Then move in."

Darra realized she was chewing on her braid and made a disgusted face. She flung it behind her shoulder. "Talk about an easy takeover."

"The question is, do we still move the Radnorans onto the Avoni transports?" Anakin asked. "We need to tell Galen this news. Maybe there's a way to delay the process until we can get more information."

"Not so fast," Darra said. "Ferus and I discovered something. The factory that made those prototype droids belongs to Galen and his sister Curi."

"Isn't it too much of a coincidence that there were security lapses at both factories?" Ferus asked. He swung one powerful leg over a chair and sat astride it.

Thoughtfully, Tru leaned back in his chair. He wrapped both his rubbery legs around each other several times, then crossed his ankles. "So Galen could be involved in the release of the droids," he said. "Or even the original industrial accident."

"Or Curi," Darra said. "Or both. Or neither. It could be an employee of theirs. Or an ex-employee. In other words, it could be anyone on this planet. And we have to find them in less than an hour! Not too much of a problem for a first mission." She reached for her braid again.

Ferus leaned over and slipped his hand into Tru's pocket. He tossed Darra a piece of figda candy. "No stress, Darra."

"We have threads, but no patterns," Anakin said. "Our Masters could be in danger. They don't know about Curi's connection to the Prototype Droids. She could be dangerous. We have to go over to the Isolation Sector and warn them."

"Hold on," Ferus said. His dark eyebrows lowered. "First of all, we were ordered to remain here, no matter what. We've been taught to heed our Masters — it's an important part of the Jedi Order."

"But things have changed," Anakin argued.

"And second, there are no bio-iso suits for us," Ferus added.

Anakin lifted his chin. "I'm not afraid. If my Master is in danger, I'll go. You can stay here and be safe."

For the first time, Anakin saw Ferus flush with anger. "This isn't a bravery contest, Anakin. Think like a Jedi."

"Don't give me orders!" Anakin shot back hotly.

"Our first duty is to the citizens of Radnor!" Ferus snapped.

Darra stepped in between them. "Okay, ferrocrete heads, let's calm down. We're supposed to work together, remember? Time is running out for the citizens of this planet. Let's focus on that."

"It's him!" Anakin and Ferus exclaimed together.

Darra's lips quirked. "Ah. At last you agree on something."

"Anakin is right. Our Masters could be in danger," Tru said. Anakin started to speak, but he held up a hand. "Ferus is also right. We must think like Jedi. And that means we must trust our Masters. We can't assume that they haven't discovered the same information that we have. We must proceed with the mission. If we have to cross over to the Isolation Sector, we will. But not yet."

"What do you suggest?" Darra asked.

"If the Radnorans remain on the planet, they will die," Tru said. "Therefore, we must allow the Avoni to transport them off-planet. But we must foil the invasion somehow."

"Four Padawans are going to foil an invasion from an entire planet?" Darra asked. She glanced at Ferus. "If you say no stress, I'll bite you."

"Okay, some stress," Ferus said with a worried smile.

They could see outside the windows of the communication center that the population of the Clear Sector was beginning to report to the evacuation points. So far things were going smoothly. But as time ran out, that could change.

"Our first step is to follow through and make sure the evacuation takes place peacefully," Ferus said. "We have to monitor the two checkpoints. Galen gave us the locations. Let's go."

Anakin trailed after the others. Once again the

Padawans split into teams to cover the two evacuation points. He headed for his designated spot with Tru. So far the lines were proceeding with little incident. Names were being checked off on datapads. The skiffs from the ferry ship had not yet arrived. There was little he and Tru could do. Anakin still wasn't happy with their decision.

"We have to find out what's really going on," Anakin said restlessly to Tru. "Our Masters could be in danger."

"It doesn't seem in character for them to just give up," Tru said.

"Our Masters?"

"The raiders," Tru mused. "Think of all the goods in that warehouse. They went to a lot of trouble to steal it. Remember the Manikons? No thief likes to leave their plunder behind."

"Why are you worrying about the raiders?" Anakin asked. "They're the least of our problems."

"Maybe they're part of our problem, only we don't know it," Tru said. "They have access to the evacuation files. They've been able to breach security and steal some major Battle Droids. We know they're connected to the evacuation effort somehow. What if —"

"They're connected to the Avoni?" Anakin asked.

Tru shrugged. "Maybe. It's worth checking out. Considering the greed of the raiders and their willingness to take advantage of their devastated fellow citizens, they'd hardly leave the planet without all the things they stole."

"You're right," Anakin said excitedly. "They might return to that warehouse." He eyed Tru. "Ferus won't like it."

"As you keep pointing out, Ferus is not our leader," Tru said. "So let's go."

Anakin felt a surge of excitement as he and Tru hurried through the streets to the warehouse. This was more like it. Jedi didn't sit passively by and wait for events to unfold. They made things happen. Tru understood that.

The population of Tacto was beginning to spill out, carrying bundles of belongings. Most citizens had blasters strapped to their waists. Tensions ran high. Everyone was intent on sticking up for themselves and their own family. No one seemed to be helping anyone else. Each Radnoran was focused on his or her place on the evacuation ship and getting there as quickly as possible.

Anakin wasn't sure how long he and Tru would be willing to wait at the warehouse. They really shouldn't have left their posts at all. The Force was dark on this planet. Violence could erupt at any time.

But they were lucky. When they slipped inside the warehouse, they found one of the raiders already there.

He was loading a gravsled with stolen goods as quickly as he could. Because of his haste, he stacked the goods clumsily. Some durasteel bins fell off the back of the gravsled, scattering their contents.

"Need some help?" Anakin asked impulsively.

He and Tru activated their lightsabers and stood before the raider. They knew they would not have to use them.

The Radnoran was small and slight. He looked from Anakin to Tru and back again. Then he tried to smile.

"Greetings. The name is Ruuin. My buddy told me that he left some of his things in this warehouse. Gave me a key, so I —"

"Save it." Anakin deactivated his lightsaber. "Time's up. The evacuation is beginning. You can get aboard a ship —"

"Or we can stick you in a detention cell," Tru said.

"And things are so confusing around here, we just might forget to get you out before the winds shift," Anakin said.

Ruuin's eyes darted nervously. "C'mon. You wouldn't do that. You're Jedi."

"Technically, we're not," Anakin said. "We're *training* to be Jedi."

"There's quite a difference, actually," Tru said. He shrugged. "We're just learning the rules."

"So let me think. Is it against Jedi rules to leave a suspect imprisoned when we know a deadly toxin is in the air?" Anakin frowned, pretending to ponder. "You have any idea, Tru?"

"I think I skipped that class," Tru said.

"Wise guys. I always meet up with wise guys," Ruuin said under his breath. "All right, all right. What do you want to know?"

"Who are you working for?" Anakin asked.

"How do I know? Some guy," the Radnoran said. He quickly put his hands up in protest as both Anakin and Tru took a step toward him. "I'm telling the truth. I was paid a wage and a share of the spoils. The guy's name is Nonce, if that helps you. If you were security police, you'd know him. He's been in detention most of his life. But somebody hired *him.* I don't know who. Now can I go?"

"How did you get access to the evacuation plans?" Anakin asked.

"I didn't. Nonce did. And I don't know how he got them. *Now* can I go?"

"If you stayed around long enough to raid all those homes and businesses, how could you be sure to get a place for the evacuation?" Tru asked.

There was a subtle shift in Ruuin's gaze. He didn't look away. But something changed. Anakin knew he was about to lie.

"We would have been done in time."

"No, you wouldn't," Anakin said. "And you wouldn't endanger yourself and your new riches by taking a chance. So what was the plan? How were you going to get off-planet?"

"The same way everyone else is," Ruuin said. "Those ferry ships. Can I go now?"

Anakin didn't know what to do. It was obvious that Ruuin wasn't going to tell them the truth. He was more afraid of someone else than he was of the Padawans.

Suddenly, Tru reached over and snatched Ruuin's datapad from his belt. "Maybe this will tell us something."

"Hey! Hey! That's my property!"

Anakin glanced at the stolen plunder around them. "Do you really think you're in a position to complain?"

Tru was busily clicking keys. "Look," he said to Anakin, tilting the datapad toward him. "See these co-ordinates? This must be a landing site. And it doesn't match the ones we know for the ferry ships."

"You have an escape plan," Anakin told Ruuin. "Let me tell you something. You're not going to make it. You're not going to make it onto a ship at all. Let me tell you something else." He took a step closer to Ruuin. "You have much more to fear from the Jedi than you do from anyone else. Even the Avoni."

"The Avoni?" Ruuin's tongue darted out nervously. "I never mentioned the Avoni. Look, you've got to let me go, all right? You don't understand the penalty I'm facing. I could be imprisoned for treason." He stopped suddenly.

"Treason," Anakin said slowly. "That means there is another planetary government involved."

"Like the Avoni," Tru said.

Ruuin wiped his perspiring forehead. "All right. Yes, it was the Avoni. The coordinates are for another Avoni ship. They're airlifting the raiders off-planet. They don't want us to get caught here. We need to leave before the Senate ships arrive. They promised us that no matter what happens, we'll get off. They backed our raids. They wanted as much disruption and panic to spread as possible. We're all supposed to get houses and money once we get to Avon."

"Didn't you ask yourself why the Avoni were doing all this?" Tru asked, disgusted. "Were you just going to allow them to invade your planet?"

"I don't ask questions," Ruuin said. "I'm a thief, not a philosopher."

"The panic would distract the population even further," Tru murmured to Anakin. "They wouldn't have time to figure out what the Avoni were planning."

Anakin nodded. He turned to Ruuin. "Who was Nonce's contact? How did you get those prototype droids? Who is the contact with the Avoni?" he rapped out.

"I don't know anything," Ruuin said desperately. "I'm just a thief. I'm nobody. There's no one left to talk to. *Now* can I go?"

CHAPTER SIXTEEN

Curi's courageous test to remove her bio-iso suit soon confirmed that there was no longer any danger from the toxin. Additional testing proved it.

All the Jedi removed their suits. It was a relief to Obi-Wan to breathe the air again. Without the constricting suit, the Jedi would be able to fight more effectively, should they need to.

"We need to head back to Clear Sector immediately," Obi-Wan said. "If we can stop the evacuation, we can stop any planned takeover by the Avoni. They're expecting an unpopulated planet."

"You know what this means about the comm systems, don't you?" Soara said. "The Avoni must be jamming the planet. It's the only explanation."

The other Jedi nodded. They had all come to the same conclusion.

They could do no more in Isolation Sector. Curi had found two functioning speeders for them. They split into teams and took off through the empty city, heading for the outskirts and the fastest route to the Clear Sector.

Despite the danger of the coming invasion, Obi-Wan felt relief that he would get to see Anakin again at last. He was anxious to see how his Padawan had fared.

"You look relieved," Siri said, giving him a quick glance as she piloted the speeder. "I am, too."

"You didn't seem very worried."

"When do I ever seem worried?" Siri said with a short laugh. "I just hide things better than you do, that's all. Sometimes I wonder if you expect me to have any feelings at all, Obi-Wan."

It was true. Obi-Wan did not often look beneath Siri's cool confidence. He should have known better.

As they reached the vast plain outside the city, Siri increased her speed. "Things always came easily to Ferus at the Temple," she remarked. "His gifts helped him sail through his classes. His good nature won him many friends. But you and I know that the galaxy teaches us harder lessons."

"Yes," Obi-Wan said. "We know this to be true."

"So I worry about the day Ferus discovers this, too,"

Siri said. "Failure is part of being a Jedi, too. The one who does not have to work hard for his gifts will one day fail, as we all do. He will try his hardest, he will sacrifice everything he has to give, and still he will not win. I suspect his failure will be rougher than it needs to be. I wait for that day, and I worry."

Obi-Wan feared the same for Anakin. Siri had put into words a certain dread he carried in his heart.

And he had congratulated himself for overcoming his old rivalry with Siri! Obi-Wan shook his head, smiling. Obviously traces of that rivalry remained. Otherwise he would have confided in her.

"What is it?" Siri asked, catching his smile.

"Remind me to stop underestimating you," he said.

She grinned. "Gladly."

"And thank you."

Siri turned her attention to the controls. She never acknowledged thanks or compliments. But Obi-Wan knew the moment had added to their friendship.

He saw a speck on the horizon, and his attention sharpened. The surge in the Force told Obi-Wan that the speck was not one of the native uizani birds of Radnor.

"To our right," he said to Siri over the noise of the airspeeder.

She nodded. Obi-Wan contacted Ry-Gaul on his

comlink and alerted him to the speck, which was now growing into a black shape.

"Definitely some kind of transport," Siri said.

The dark presence in the Force was growing. Obi-Wan felt it like a wave against his skin.

"Strange," he said. "It looks like a smaller version of an MTT." He was familiar with the Multi Troop Transport ships from his dealings with the Trade Federation. Battle Droids could be compressed and loaded into the ship with no wasted space.

"An MTT? I think you might be right. Well, now we have the answer to my question," Siri said grimly. "We know how they are transporting Battle Droids. The MTT must have been in the cargo hold of one of the ferry ships."

"That's why the Avoni officer ordered a lockdown of the cargo holds," Obi-Wan guessed.

"We'd better get off these coordinates." Siri deftly turned the airspeeder to the right. Behind her, Ry-Gaul made the same turn. "I think I remember some ground canyons due south of us. Can you find them?"

Obi-Wan entered their coordinates on the onboard computer. "You're right. We're only a few kilometers away. We can hide there and see what's going on. Before we stop the evacuation we should find out exactly what we're up against. It shouldn't take long." He entered the new coordinates, then quickly contacted Ry-Gaul and Soara to tell them the new plan.

Siri pushed the engines faster. They were close to the ground and small enough that they should avoid detection. They assumed the transport was headed for the city of Aubendo.

"The ship is turning," Obi-Wan said suddenly.

"That's odd," Siri muttered. She glanced over her shoulder, then pushed the engines harder. "Can you get a fix on it?"

Obi-Wan aimed a macrolaser tracker at the ship. Within seconds, the airspeeder computer had mapped out the probable destination of the ship. The coordinates matched where they were heading.

"Either it's following us, or it's heading to the same canyon area," Obi-Wan told Siri. "Let's try an experiment."

Quickly, he entered new coordinates into the shipboard computer. Siri changed direction. After a few moments, the ship changed as well.

"It *is* following us," Siri said. "Why? What would an MTT want with two tiny airspeeders?"

"Unless they know the Jedi are aboard," Obi-Wan said.

Siri gave him a quick glance, the wind whipping her hair against her cheek. "Curi?"

"Maybe. Or we could have been under surveillance. Our only hope is to lose it in those canyons. Those ships are too big to maneuver the way we can."

"We'll have to get to the canyons first," Siri murmured. The engines were on full, and the MTT was gaining.

Obi-Wan answered his comlink and heard Soara's clipped tone. "They must know we're Jedi."

"Yes. We can lose it in the canyons."

"Let's hope so. Those MTTs can carry a full platoon of droids."

Obi-Wan cut the communication. The ship was gaining on them. He wasn't concerned. The canyons were only a few kilometers away. They should make it. He had complete confidence in Siri's ability as a pilot. The bulky transport would not be able to follow them.

He wasn't concerned . . . *so why am I concerned?* Obi-Wan wondered, shaking his head at his lapse in logic.

"Something's wrong," he said.

"There you go again," Siri said. "Stating the obvious."

"So you feel it, too?"

"I do."

"They could be herding us toward the canyons because they know they could trap us there."

"They could. But we have no choice. We don't have another strategy," Siri said. "There's nothing between here and Tacto. No place for us to hide."

The canyons were ahead. They could see the odd zigzag tracing of them in the ground. It wasn't until they were on top of them that they could see that the lines on the ground were actually deep fissures. Siri aimed the airspeeder down into their depths. The sky went gray as the sun disappeared.

The fissure widened as they dropped, and they found themselves in a large underground canyon. There were offshoots to the sides, but they were too narrow even for an airspeeder.

Ry-Gaul hugged their rear. The MTT zoomed downward, still chasing them.

"They have a plan, all right," Siri said between her teeth as she dove down.

Obi-Wan wished they had a more nimble transport. The airspeeder was meant to travel on repulsorlift engines along the surface of a planet. It had a limited ability to dive and maneuver.

The MTT was almost on them now. Obi-Wan was uncomfortably aware that MTTs were often equipped with proton torpedos.

"What I wouldn't give for a deflector shield," Siri muttered.

Suddenly the canyon wall next to them exploded. Rocks and debris slammed into the airspeeder. Siri had trouble hanging on to the controls.

Behind them, Ry-Gaul and Soara were also in trouble. A blast from the MTT had hit their rear. They were falling through the air, trailing black smoke. Ry-Gaul fought to regain power.

"They're going down!" Obi-Wan shouted.

Obi-Wan reached out with the Force, knowing it was useless. He could not stop an airspeeder from crashing. Helplessly, he watched it begin to spiral.

"Hang on!" Siri shouted. She put their airspeeder into a steep dive. Underneath her hands, the controls vibrated and the whole craft shook. She was pushing the craft to its maximum — and beyond.

Siri turned sharply to the left, slipping under the other airspeeder. At the exact moment they were underneath, Ry-Gaul and Soara leaped.

They landed on the rear of the speeder, sending it tilting crazily. Ry-Gaul and Soara released their cable hooks, fastening themselves to the craft as it bucked and rolled. Siri's face was set with determination as she battled with the out-of-control speeder.

Ground loomed up at them. Canyon walls rushed past. Ahead was a sheer cliff. Siri tried to slow the craft, but the engines were stuck.

"Cut the power!" Obi-Wan shouted.

Siri shut down the engines. With a piercing whine, they cut out. The speeder bounced off the ground, then spun wildly. Soara and Ry-Gaul desperately hung onto their cables. Obi-Wan was thrown from his door against Siri. His head slammed back against the seat.

The speeder suddenly smashed against the canyon wall, then came to a stop.

Obi-Wan tasted blood in his mouth, but he knew he was unhurt. He looked over at Siri. She winced, but she nodded to let him know she was all right. Soara was trying to pick herself up, but her leg was at an awkward angle. Ry-Gaul supported her and helped her rise.

The Jedi did not hesitate. They did not even have time to wait until their heads were clear. The MTT was zooming down toward them, laser cannons firing.

Obi-Wan and Siri leaped off the speeder and ran for cover. Ry-Gaul supported Soara and hustled her toward shelter. Obi-Wan found a small passageway between sheer canyon walls. He darted inside and the others followed.

Ry-Gaul leaned down to examine Soara's leg. "Not broken."

Soara tried to smile. "At last some good news."

"Can you walk?" Obi-Wan asked.

"Yes," Soara said, her face white with pain.

"No," Ry-Gaul said gently. "But I will help you."

They followed the twisting trail, moving as fast as they could despite Soara's injury.

"I doubt they'll unload the droids here," Siri said.

"If this is an invasion, they'll want to get on with it," Soara said through clenched teeth. "Why waste time on four Jedi? Maybe they'll just give up and go away."

"This trail is doubling back on itself," Obi-Wan said suddenly. "It's going to bring us back to where we started."

"Great," Siri said. "I missed that MTT."

Obi-Wan inched close to the edge of the wall. He looked out.

The MTT had landed in a clear space a few hundred meters away. The ramp lowered. As Obi-Wan watched, troop after troop of Prototype Droids marched down.

"They are unloading the droids," he said. "They aren't giving up."

CHAPTER SEVENTEEN

Anakin and Tru managed to find one of the few security officers left on the planet. They left Ruuin in his care.

"I wouldn't be surprised if he bribes or talks his way out of custody," Anakin said, watching as Ruuin walked away with the officer, talking quickly and gesturing with his short, stubby arms.

"It doesn't matter," Tru answered. "We have proof that Radnor is being invaded. We'd better talk to the others."

"Sure, so Ferus can tell us what to do," Anakin grumbled.

"Well, what do *you* think we should do?" Tru asked as they hurried toward the checkpoint Ferus and Darra were guarding.

"I think Galen is behind this, and we should confront him," Anakin said. "He can tell us exactly what the Avoni are planning. Then we can figure out how to foil it."

"Somehow I doubt it will be that easy," Tru said.

"I do, too," Anakin agreed. "But I can't think of anything else."

They reached Darra and Ferus and quickly told them what they had found.

"We don't know for sure that it's Galen," Ferus said.

"We don't have time to come up with another suspect," Anakin insisted. "We have to move now. We don't know what's going on in the Isolation Sector. Our Masters could be in danger."

"Anakin is right," Darra agreed. "We won't lose anything by confronting Galen."

"Let's go," Ferus declared.

As if it was his idea, Anakin thought.

The four Padawans hurried to the command center. Galen was just tossing a small survival kit into his airspeeder.

"Going somewhere?" Anakin asked.

"Of course I am," Galen answered. "As soon as everyone is safely off the planet."

"You seem to be in a special hurry," Darra observed.

Galen gave an exasperated sigh. "What are you getting at now?"

"We have solid information that the planet Avon was behind the raids and also the theft of those Prototype Droids," Anakin said. "And we think you know something about it."

Galen chuckled, shaking his head. "You kids sure come up with some incredible theories. I've been trying to *help* the citizens of Radnor!"

"What about the original toxic accident?" Ferus asked. "And the theft of the droids? Both things happened at your facilities."

"It's called bad luck," Galen said. "I'm one of the top scientists on Radnor. Maybe someone targeted me. And as soon as all this is over, we'll be going over our safety procedures very carefully. But I'm not responsible. I've been risking my life by staying here. I could have left long ago. I had the money. My sister and I decided to stay to help our fellow citizens. Why are you accusing me?"

Now Galen looked hurt, not angry. Anakin did not pick up anything amiss. He wished Obi-Wan were here. He was not yet adept at reading the true motives of other beings.

Anakin remembered Ruuin's anxiousness to get away. No doubt he had a rendezvous time with the

Avoni as well as a rendezvous point. Maybe Galen had the same problem.

"I say we just hold him until the Avoni ships take off," Anakin told the others. "He can wait here with us for the Senate ships."

Tru's silver eyes flickered as he understood Anakin's strategy. "I agree."

"This is ridiculous!" Galen exploded. Finally they had cracked his wounded composure. "I refuse, after all I've done, to subject myself to these suspicions."

He jumped inside the airspeeder and revved the engine. But he hadn't counted on the quick reflexes of the Padawans. Anakin reached over and shut off the engine as Tru jumped in and accessed the onboard computer. He read out the coordinates that flashed on the screen. They were the same as Ruuin's.

"I'm sorry, Galen," Anakin said. "We now have proof. Those are the coordinates of an Avoni landing site. You are going to be airlifted off-planet."

"Yes, so what?" Galen bellowed. "Along with everyone else!"

"I don't think so. I think you cut a special deal with the invaders. You and your conspirators would have had new lives on Avon — thanks to your betrayal of your planet."

A small, shocked voice came from behind them. "No."

Anakin turned. A small woman with features similar to Galen's stood in the doorway. He recognized Galen's sister Curi from the hologram Galen had received the day they'd arrived. "It can't be true. Galen? Is it true?"

"Of course not, Curi," Galen said. "These Jedi are children. What do they know?"

Darra ignored Galen's comment. "Did you leave our Masters in the Isolation Sector?" she asked urgently.

Curi tore her sorrowful gaze from her brother and faced the Padawans. "They were on their way here. The toxin is no longer dangerous. It has a short half-life, we've just discovered. The winds will bring no danger to Tacto."

"And our Masters?" Darra asked. "Where are they now?"

"They are in great danger," Curi said. "They are pinned down by the Avoni invaders outside the city of Aubendo in the ground canyon fields. Dol Heep had them under surveillance. I discovered that he had placed tracking devices in my transports. When I found out I went after them. I was just in time to see a large vessel force them down. They are under attack from a platoon of Battle Droids. *Our* Battle Droids," she added, with a glance at Galen.

"How can we trust her?" Ferus asked the others in

a low tone. "What if she and Galen are in league together? What if they're trying to get us out of the Clear
Sector so they can take off?"

The Padawans looked at one another, confusion on
their faces. Yes, Curi could be lying. Galen definitely
was. Who could they trust?

Trust yourself. Breathe in your instinct. Then act.

Anakin closed his eyes for a moment. He touched
the river stone in his pocket, sliding his fingers over its
warmth. He reached out to the Force, to a place that he
knew well. He felt a distant tug — Obi-Wan. Yes, his
Master was in danger. And Curi . . . Curi was telling the
truth.

Unease was still on his fellow Padawans' faces. But
Anakin locked eyes with Ferus. "We can't take a chance
with our Masters' lives."

Ferus hesitated only a fraction, surprised at the
depth of Anakin's contact with the Force. "You're right.
Let's go."

CHAPTER EIGHTEEN

The Padawans commandeered Galen's airspeeder. The four of them squeezed inside. Curi gave them the coordinates of where she had last seen the Avoni transport and the Jedi.

"Look at all these Radnorans in bio-isolation suits," Darra observed. "I sure hope Curi is telling the truth, or we'll be in for a big surprise when the winds shift."

Darra spoke lightly, but no one felt entirely easy about their decision. Even Anakin was a little worried. He was betting everything on his intuition. If he was wrong, the consequences would be severe. He could die, along with the other Padawans.

I'm not wrong.

He could feel Ferus's eyes on him. He kept his gaze

forward as he piloted the craft. He wasn't about to re-treat now.

Ahead they saw the energy gate that led to the Isolation Sector. Curi had given them the coordinates to bypass it. Anakin entered them into a signal beam and the energy gate opened. They zoomed through.

For a moment, they all held their breath. Then Ferus took a deep breath. Darra did the same.

"Well, there's no turning back now," she said.

Ferus accessed the mapping device on the shipboard computer. He studied the ground canyon site. "There are several access points," he said.

"We have to assume that they're probably still very close to where Curi saw them," Darra said. "She said their speeders were destroyed."

"She also said the transport following them was quite large," Tru added. "So if we take a narrow route through the canyons, we might have the element of surprise."

"We're going to need more than surprise if that transport was filled with Prototype Droids," Ferus remarked. "Not only that, the transport probably has some sort of blaster cannons."

"If you're trying to raise our confidence level, it's not working," Darra said.

"We're coming up on the ground canyons," Ferus warned.

Anakin slowed down slightly. Ahead he only saw what looked like scribble markings on the ground. Then he realized the markings revealed deep cracks in the ground surface.

Ferus read out a coordinate. "Take that route," he said. "It will bring us close to where Curi saw our Masters."

Anakin zoomed down the canyon. He hugged the canyon walls, going as fast as he dared. By the look on Ferus's face, it was faster than the other Padawan would like. Anakin pushed the engines up a notch. He knew he was in complete control.

Ahead he saw the large, hulking shape of the Avoni transport ship. It was idling, its repulsorlift engines on low, keeping it a few meters off the ground. Dust rose around it in a filmy cloud. Anakin grew excited.

"I've seen that kind of transport before," he said. "It was years ago, in the Trade Federation battle for Naboo. This is a slightly smaller version of an MTT — a Multi Troop Transport. They store Battle Droids and are usually piloted by two droids."

"They also have heavy frontal armor. The ship itself

can be a weapon." Tru looked uneasy. "They can go through rock walls."

"It looks like this one already did," Darra said, swallowing hard.

A solid wall of rock had been splintered into fragments. Droids littered the ground.

"Our Masters must have battled there," Ferus said in a hushed tone.

Anakin hovered near the sight, careful to keep out of sight of the MTT's bridge. They saw no evidence of their Masters.

"I hear blaster fire," Darra said suddenly. "We're close."

Then Anakin could hear it, too. He placed his hands back on the controls, ready to zoom ahead.

"Wait!" Ferus commanded.

Annoyed, Anakin turned to him. "What now? More *planning*?"

"Yes," Ferus said steadily. "If we rush in there without a plan, we won't be much help to them."

"What kind of a plan do we need?" Anakin asked. "They're being attacked by droids! We go in and help them!"

Darra groaned. "I thought the worst thing about being on this mission was protein cubes for breakfast. Now I know it's you two. Ferus, what are you thinking?"

"How many droids did the MTT on Naboo hold?" Ferus asked Anakin.

"I don't remember," Anakin said. "Over a hundred, I think."

"One hundred and twelve," Tru said softly.

"And this is only a little smaller," Ferus said. "So let's say it holds about fifty to seventy droids, at least. What are the chances we can battle that many with our lightsabers?"

Darra swallowed. "I can't tell you how much I hate to hear the odds before a battle."

"So what are you saying?" Anakin asked. "We call for more Jedi?"

"Or more lightsabers," Darra said.

Ferus shook his head. "Of course not. We just need to think, that's all. We have a couple of advantages. One is surprise. The other is the fact that you and Tru seem to know a lot about that transport."

Anakin nodded. He had explored one on Naboo after the battle.

"The question is, how do we get aboard?" Ferus asked.

"Can you deactivate the droids from the MTT?" Darra asked.

Anakin shook his head. "No, they're controlled from either the landing ship or from orbit."

"No stress with that," Ferus said. "If you get aboard, can you pilot the ship?"

"I can pilot anything," Anakin said flatly.

"Didn't you say that the ship is also a weapon?" Ferus asked.

The four Padawans looked at one another.

"Of course," Anakin said. "If we control the ship, we control the battle."

"There's the deployment hatch," Tru said. "But the release valve is on the bridge."

"I think the only way is —" Anakin began.

"You're right," Tru said. "But we'd have to do it —"

"Exactly. But the venting system —"

"So we don't have to worry about being seen." Tru nodded rapidly. "Okay, that's it, then."

"That's *what*?" Darra cried. "Are you two speaking some weird language from the Outer Rim?"

Anakin turned to her. "The MTT is designed by the Baktoid workshop. The Trade Federation buys most of their ships, but they rotate out the old ones and sell them off to various planets. I'm betting that's what this transport is. Which means that its exhaust and cooling system is vented straight down toward the ground. There's some unusually large vents on the bottom. That's why you see all that dust around it. It's kicked up by the wind coming out of the ship."

"So the dust will give us cover," Tru said. "And the vents are big enough. We can just climb up them to get aboard."

"Won't the wind blow you back?" Ferus asked.

"If the ship was moving, it would," Anakin said. "But the engines are idling. The ship is in passive mode. We shouldn't have too much trouble."

"We've got another problem," Darra said. "If you get control of the ship, our Masters won't know it. They'll most likely attack the ship when it comes toward them."

"That's why we have to split up," Ferus said. "Darra, you and I have to make contact with the Masters while Anakin and Tru steal the ship. We have to get the droids to follow us to an ambush." He looked at Anakin and Tru. "Does that sound okay to you?"

It was the first time Ferus had asked his opinion. Anakin nodded. "Sounds like a good plan."

"We have an agreement," Darra muttered. "Remind me to declare this an annual holiday once we get back to the Temple."

She leaned over and accessed a map to the canyons. Quickly she flipped through different sites. Then she stabbed at the viewscreen with a finger. "There. If you can maneuver the ship there, we can bring the droids through that smaller canyon and out into the clearing. Then we've got them."

The four Padawans looked at one another, exhilarated. They were going to save their Masters.

"No stress with that," Ferus said confidently.

"Completely," Anakin echoed.

There was a pause. After the initial confidence, the weight of the task ahead settled on them.

"May the Force be with us," Tru said quietly.

Ferus and Darra exited the airspeeder. Hugging the rocks, they started off through the canyon toward the sound of blaster fire.

Anakin and Tru headed in the opposite direction. They paused in the shelter of a rock to watch the MTT and its inhabitants. They could just make out the heads of the droid pilots. They rotated in constant surveillance.

"Anakin —"

"I know," Anakin said. "It's a question of timing."

"I was going to say, we just have to run really, really fast," Tru said, flashing him a quick grin.

"Aim for the dust cloud."

"Right."

Anakin fitted a filter mask over his nose and pulled his hood up. Tru did the same. They slipped goggles out from their utility belts and pulled them on.

As soon as the droids' heads turned the opposite way and they were no longer in their sight line, they ran.

Anakin felt the Force rise around him from the rocks

and dust. It seemed to push him faster, allowing him to dive into the sand cloud kicked up by the ship's exhaust.

Anakin hated sand. He had seen and tasted too much of it while a slave on Tatooine. Now it filtered through the dust mask and settled in his mouth. He could barely see. He could sense rather than see Tru beside him.

He held up a hand, feeling along the underside of the ship. The sand and dust were so disorienting it was hard to visualize where he was. Then he felt a raised piece of metal. Could it be the repulsor cooling fins? He ran a hand along one ridge, then another. That meant the vents were just ahead.

The wind blasts were stronger than he'd anticipated. The thought of his Master pinned down by a platoon of droids pushed him on. He could feel Tru battling the wind beside him.

Anakin reached the vents. He hoisted himself up and inside, spreading his hands out to support himself against the rounded walls and bracing himself with his feet. He would be able to move sideways up the shaft. The blast of wind was warm, but not hot. It pushed against him, but he was able to move slowly up the shaft, meter by meter, first using one hand and foot, then the other. Tru was directly beneath him.

Halfway up the vent, Anakin felt as though his legs were made of ferrocrete and his arm muscles had begun to shake. One foot slid and he almost lost his position and fell. He felt Tru touch his back. Anakin turned, and Tru motioned to him. He would lead the way.

Anakin curled himself into a ball so that Tru could crawl past him. As soon as Anakin was behind Tru, he felt the wind lessen. Tru's flexible arms and legs were much more suited to scrambling up the vent. His body now acted as a shield. It gave Anakin a chance to re-store his own strength. *This is what Obi-Wan means,* he thought suddenly. *I do not always have to prove I can lead. Sometimes someone else can do the job better.*

At last the vent opened out into the engine room, next to the humming repulsorlift generators. Anakin and Tru collapsed on the floor, trying to catch their breath.

"Whew. Some stress with that," Tru said, gasping.

They got to their feet and looked around the engine room.

"I'd say —" Tru started.

"That way," Anakin agreed.

Once they left the engine room, they had to turn sideways to navigate the corridor. Every centimeter of space was used on the vessel to pack in droids. They squeezed past the empty troop deployment racks and climbed a narrow metal staircase to the bridge. Outside the bridge door they activated their lightsabers. Taking a breath for concentration, they accessed the door and burst inside.

The droids swiveled, instantly taking in the danger. Their arms moved forward in blast mode.

Anakin and Tru were faster. They somersaulted in the air and came down with their lightsabers, each neatly slicing a droid in half.

Anakin kicked aside the droid and immediately moved to the controls. He studied them.

"Can't help you out here," Tru said. "I never got this far in the manual. Got too bored."

"It's okay. These controls are basic. You'd better strap into the copilot's seat. It might be rough going."

Experimentally, Anakin eased the controls forward. The ship gave a great lurch. Tru hadn't had a chance to sit, and he went flying. He landed on the floor.

"*Might* be rough?" Tru picked himself up, kicked the droid out of the way, and sat in the copilot's seat.

The next time Anakin eased the controls, the ship moved more smoothly. He took it slow for several meters, getting used to the way the ship handled. This was no nimble starfighter. This was a lumbering beast.

He would have to navigate around this canyon,

through a narrower passage, and then get the beast down a smaller passage into the large clearing. Everything depended on him and Tru getting there. No one had said it, but everyone was aware that if Anakin could not maneuver the ship there, the Jedi would be trapped in the canyon with a platoon of droids — and no way out.

Anakin turned the ship into the narrower passage. He accelerated, searching for the passage Darra had marked.

After a few minutes Tru spoke. "We should have passed the turning by now."

"I know. Let's just . . ." Anakin's words died. Ahead, he saw only solid rock. They had come to the end of the passage. There was no way into the clearing.

"This can't be," Anakin said. He pounded the controls with his fists. "It can't be!" There was no passage. Darra had read the map wrong. They had failed, and his Master was trapped. He shouldn't have listened to Ferus. He should have —

"Can you back this thing up?" Tru asked.

Anakin tried to quiet the ranting voices in his head. "What?"

"The passage to the clearing must be blocked. It was probably a rockslide. Remember we passed that area of the wall that had all that sheared rock in the road?"

With a swift motion, Anakin reversed the engines and zoomed backward. He stopped the MTT where Tru had indicated. A passage had been here once, but it was hard to tell. Huge boulders now blocked it.

"Is there any other way to the clearing?" Tru asked.

Anakin shook his head. "They could be in there by now. We've got to get through that rock."

"Can the MTT handle it?"

Anakin gripped the controls. They could get stuck halfway through. The rocks could collapse and bury them alive. "I don't know. But if we don't try, our Masters are doomed."

CHAPTER NINETEEN

The Jedi crouched behind a screen of boulders and splintered rock. They had been pinned down for two hours. They had fought off three assaults from the droids. The droids held a position across the canyon where they could fire at any flicker of movement from the Jedi. Ry-Gaul had a blaster wound to the shoulder. Soara's ankle had swelled, but she'd fashioned a makeshift crutch from a felled droid's leg. A splintering rock had cut Siri over the eye. And they were all exhausted.

Over the course of the day they had kept moving from one small canyon to the next, but the smaller canyons were a maze that always led back to the large clearing and the MTT. That was what the Avoni had known. They had known they would be able to run the Jedi down until they were exhausted.

The droids were relentless, and there were so many of them. They estimated seventy to eighty. They had taken out at least twenty, maybe more. But there were at least fifty still out there, and no doubt fresh reserves would arrive. While the Jedi were pinned down, the Avoni would conduct their invasion. The Jedi Masters had not spoken of it, but they knew they were each thinking of their Padawans.

"Our only chance is to get back to the MTT," Obi-Wan said to the others. "We have to capture the ship. It's the only way out."

"Capture an MTT?" Soara asked. "It's an armored tank."

"There's got to be a way." *If Anakin were here, he would know how,* Obi-Wan thought. Anakin knew his way around every ship that was ever built. He made it his business to know.

"Hold it," Siri said. "Look!"

Obi-Wan followed her pointing finger. To his surprise, he saw Ferus and Darra heading for them, moving from rock to rock for cover. The droids turned to fire at them, keeping up a steady barrage.

A pang shot through Obi-Wan. *Where was Anakin?*

If something had happened to him, I would know it. I would feel it.

Ferus and Darra ran the last hundred meters, dodging blaster fire and blocking it with their lightsabers. They dived behind the rocks with the Jedi.

"So glad you could join us," Soara said.

"Thought you might have missed us," Darra said with a grin. Then she noted Soara's injury. "Master, you're hurt!"

"Just a minor inconvenience," Soara answered.

"Anakin and Tru are capturing the MTT," Ferus told them. "We hope. Our plan is to lure the droids to a clearing and then use the MTT to destroy them."

"How are they getting aboard the MTT?" Obi-Wan asked.

"Apparently it has large venting tunnels on its underside," Ferus said. "They said they could navigate them."

Obi-Wan nodded. It sounded dangerous, but he trusted Anakin's abilities. "How far is the rendezvous?"

"Not far. We studied the map. If we can return the way we came and get the droids to follow us down a passage, it will empty into the clearing."

"We'll have no problem with the droids following us," Obi-Wan said grimly.

"No time like the present," Ry-Gaul said.

"I was getting tired of this spot anyway," Siri said, wiping the blood off her forehead with her sleeve.

The Jedi gathered themselves for the next phase of the battle. They were exhausted, but they had reserves of strength they had not tapped. Ferus and Darra had given them a way out, and they were ready.

They rushed out together, lightsabers drawn. The Prototype Droids moved toward them, the front line blasting heavy firepower at them. The Jedi kept on the move. The two Masters were careful to ensure that Soara and Ry-Gaul were protected at all times. With his shoulder injury, Ry-Gaul could only swing the lightsaber to one side, and that was painful. Soara's limping progress was remarkably fast with the help of her makeshift crutch.

They reached the shelter of the passageway. They had just a moment to catch their breath. The droids wheeled in formation and followed.

They ran, letting the droids keep them in sight, but staying out of blaster range. Ferus and Darra led the way. They snaked through the passageway and came out into the clearing.

The droid platoon was behind them. Sheer rock was ahead of them.

"How is the MTT going to get in here?" Obi-Wan asked.

Ferus turned pale. "There was a route . . ."

Darra looked around wildly. "Where is the passage? It should be there!" She pointed to an area that appeared to be a wall of boulders.

"Rock slide," Ry-Gaul said. "See the markings there?"

"We're trapped," Soara said, glancing around quickly. "We'll have to fight them in the open." She gripped her crutch with one hand and her lightsaber with the other.

"Anakin will reach us." Obi-Wan's voice was steady.

"Through sheer rock?" Soara asked.

The droids poured into the clearing. The Jedi stood, ready to face them. Ready to face death. Whatever came, they were ready. Darra's hand trembled slightly as she held her lightsaber, but she moved resolutely to cover Soara's injured side.

A tremendous noise shook the canyon. The huge boulders on the side of the canyon began to tremble. Suddenly the battered MTT burst through the wall, scattering boulders like pebbles as it mowed through the canyon and headed straight for the droids. The front of the MTT was almost completely bashed in. The engines belched smoke. But the lumbering craft still moved with lurching power as it mowed down most of the entire droid platoon. What it didn't cut down immediately was reduced to scrap by blasting proton cannons. Obi-Wan had no doubt who was at the controls.

A loud banging rang through the canyon. The battered and bent hatch on top of the bridge popped open, and Anakin emerged. He waved.

"Yes," Obi-Wan said. "He will get through sheer rock. If he has to."

CHAPTER TWENTY

The Avoni had planned a bloodless invasion. Once the Jedi returned to Aubendo in the captured MTT and confronted Dol Heep, their plans were foiled. They did not have enough firepower to defeat a roused population.

"A complete misunderstanding," Dol Heep boomed. "Invasion? Hardly. We came to help Radnor. The Battle Droids were merely here for crowd control. So sorry about the malfunction." He eyed Soara's injured leg and Ry-Gaul's blaster wound. "However, I can see why you are so testy. Since there is no danger from the toxin, the Avoni will be happy to leave."

"We will be happy to escort you," Obi-Wan said firmly.

"But first, restore all communications to the planet," Siri added.

"We had nothing to do with the communication breakdown," Dol Heep said in the same hearty tone. "But out of the charity in my heart for the Radnoran people, I will speak to our tech experts and see if we can help."

Within minutes, communications were restored. While Ry-Gaul and Soara had their wounds tended, Siri contacted the Temple. The Senate ships were ordered to return to Coruscant. They suspected that there had been a sabotage of the engines, but there was no way to prove it.

The Radnorans would file a protest with the Senate, which would most likely get mired in debate and details. The Avoni would not pay for their plans for some time.

Meanwhile, Obi-Wan contacted the remaining security officers on the planet and ordered them to quickly spread the word about the safety of the planet. Radnorans could return to their homes.

"And put Galen into custody immediately," Obi-Wan added.

"He already is," the officer replied.

* * *

The Jedi arrived at the Tacto prison and were shown to a holding cell. There, Curi faced her brother across a battered metal table.

"She held a blaster on him for two hours," the security officer murmured to them. "She told him she would kill him if he tried to escape, and I guess he knew she meant it."

The Jedi stood in the doorway. Curi looked ravaged by pain and exhaustion.

"You have been a traitor to your planet," she said in a flat voice to her brother. "And you have broken my heart."

"I had no choice!" Galen said. "Don't you see I had to do what I did?"

"No," Curi said, shaking her head.

"You refused to deal with the Avoni. That made no sense! We dealt with anyone with the credits to pay. And so they threatened me."

"You could have told me."

"They told me that if I told you what they wanted — if I told anyone — they would destroy our business," Galen went on rapidly. "I had to agree to show Dol Heep the weapons plan we were developing. That's when the toxin was released. He did it before I could stop him. I got us both back to the Clear Sector before it took hold."

"So you could have brought the toxin back and endangered Tacto as well," Curi said. "It is just luck that you did not."

Galen ignored this. "Dol Heep contacted his superiors. He told me that if I kept my mouth shut about the half-life of the toxin, they would pay us money and relocate us —"

"Don't say *us*!" Curi shouted suddenly. "This is about *you*, Galen!"

"I did it for us," Galen pleaded. "They said that if I didn't do what they wanted, they would say that I was the one who released the cloud deliberately. I didn't know what to do. They asked me for the research records and for the access code to our prototype Battle Droids —"

"And they paid you money for this," Curi said bitterly. "They paid you a small fortune to betray me and yourself and your planet."

"I didn't know they were planning an invasion!"

"A *child* would have known they were planning an invasion!" Curi shouted. She stood and leaned over the table. "It is all excuses and lies. It always has been. I've never seen you so clearly. You brought me into this business. You made my life what it is. I made weapons to destroy beings and planets. I found money to fund your research into the terrible, cunning ways beings can kill other beings. I sold these weapons and put the credits in my pocket. I helped bring these things into the galaxy and I will never get the smell of death out of my nostrils. No matter what I do now, no matter where I go."

"Curi, don't. I need you! They're going to imprison me for years —"

"You are lucky they don't kill you."

Curi turned and walked out the door.

Galen turned furious eyes on the Jedi. "You see what you've done? You've poisoned her against me!"

Obi-Wan shook his head. "Your planet is in ruins. Your family is destroyed. Thousands are dead. And still you blame others. You have not learned anything."

"There is nothing to learn!" Galen shouted.

The echo of his words followed them as the Masters and Padawans walked down the hall.

They walked out into a bright morning. The devastation of the city of Tacto was revealed. The mobs had burned and rioted. Businesses were destroyed. Houses were barricaded. All air transports had been destroyed and looted for parts.

But now the Radnorans were busy returning to their homes and businesses. The sick were being cared for. The dead were being mourned.

"The Radnorans of Tacto are refusing to help any in the Isolation Sector who have survived," Ferus said.

"And they blame the Avoni for everything," Tru said. "They do not look to themselves for blame."

"Just like Galen," Darra said. "Tell me something. Are all missions this hard?"

"No," Soara said. "Some are harder."

"Neighbor turned on neighbor when the disaster occurred," Obi-Wan said. "This could have been an opportunity for generosity and sacrifice. Cowardice and violence erupted instead. This city was destroyed by greed and fear, not by a toxin."

"Not a good sign for the future of Radnor," Siri said.

"Yes, I won't be surprised if we are called here again someday," Ry-Gaul said.

The Jedi moved through the devastated streets toward their Senate transport. Obi-Wan swung into step beside Anakin.

"I am proud of you," he told him. "Not only did you act bravely, you worked well with the other Padawans. I heard how you all collaborated on the final plan to rescue us. You have learned a valuable Jedi lesson. You submitted your own will to listen to others. As a result, you gained strength."

"I was ready to rush after you to fight the droids," Anakin admitted. "It was Ferus who stopped me. He was right." *He was also lucky,* Anakin thought. The plan had almost gone awry. If Anakin had not managed to blast through the rock slide, four Jedi Masters and two Padawans would be dead.

But no one was bringing that up. Was Anakin the only one thinking it?

Obi-Wan would say it did not matter. What had happened, had happened. Jedi did not waste their time on ifs.

But Anakin couldn't look at it that way. The ifs were what intrigued him. The spaces between the rules.

If Ferus had been more lucky than right, had submitting his will been the right thing after all? He knew the question was not a Jedi question. He would not ask it of Obi-Wan.

It was his question. Only he could find the answer.

"So am I right? Do you feel you learned the Jedi lesson of submission of will? Do you understand the importance of the lesson?" Obi-Wan asked.

Anakin had to stop himself from giving away his unease. He would not lie to his Master. But had he truly submitted his will to Ferus? If he had to be honest, he would have to say no.

But he had submitted his will to Tru! Anakin recalled how in the exhaust system of the MTT, he had realized that Tru should be the one to lead. He had realized then how necessary cooperation was to the success of a mission. That had been the moment he had truly learned the Jedi lesson.

"Yes, I have learned the lesson well," he answered. He was happy he could be truthful.

Obi-Wan nodded in satisfaction and turned to board the transport.

Anakin started after him, but Ferus suddenly appeared at his side. Anakin had not sensed him nearby. "It's not the Jedi way to lie to your Master."

"Neither is eavesdropping," Anakin said, annoyed. "And I didn't lie."

Ferus studied him. The sunlight shone on the thick gold streaks in his dark hair. He did not look angry or accusatory. Merely thoughtful. "You did not tell the truth," he said. "You did not truly learn the Jedi lesson. You didn't learn anything. You are like Galen."

"That isn't so." Anakin kept his voice steady. "And it is not your business. It is my Master's business what I learn."

"Obi-Wan doesn't see you clearly," Ferus said softly. "He is a great Jedi Knight, but he is blinded by affection. But I see. And I will keep looking. I will watch you, Anakin Skywalker."

Ferus turned and strode up the ramp. Anakin had to stop himself from hurtling after him and tackling him to the floor. His body shook with rage.

Take a breath. Then another.

Anakin willed his beating heart to slow. Slowly the red mist before his eyes cleared.

I will watch you, too, Ferus. And if there is a battle between us, I will win.

ABOUT THE AUTHOR

JUDE WATSON is the *New York Times* best-selling author of the Jedi Quest and Jedi Apprentice series, as well as the Star Wars Journals *Darth Maul, Queen Amidala,* and *Princess Leia: Captive to Evil.* She currently lives in the Pacific Northwest.

LOOK FOR

JEDI QUEST

#2 THE TRAIL OF THE JEDI

From deep space, the planet Ragoon-6 lay concealed by a blue mist shimmering in the midst of a cluster of stars. As the transport descended, the mist broke into sparkling particles that swirled around the viewscreen. Then the ship broke through into a planetary atmosphere so clear it seemed as transparent as water. Glinting below was a planet as green as a flashing jewel.

Anakin Skywalker's breath caught as he leaned forward. He had never seen such a beautiful approach to a planet.

Obi-Wan Kenobi put a hand on his shoulder as he, too, leaned forward. "I had forgotten how beautiful it is."

Anakin glanced at his Master. Despite his beard, his face suddenly looked young, even younger than when Anakin had met him five years before, when Anakin was nine years old. Obi-Wan had been a Padawan then, just like Anakin was now. No doubt Obi-Wan was remembering his other trips to the planet, the ones he had taken with his own Master, Qui-Gon Jinn.

Wren Honoran, their Jedi pilot, nodded. "I always forget until the next time I see it. It takes your breath away every time."

"It's amazing that it hasn't been colonized," Anakin said.

"It was given in trust to the Senate by its own government," Obi-Wan explained. "Only small tribes of natives still inhabit it. A Senate committee handles requests to visit. Only the Jedi and small groups of beings can visit at any one time. Access is strictly controlled. That way Ragoon-6 will remain unspoiled, as the government wanted. There are no air lanes, no factories, no cities."

"The Ragoons never allowed colonizers to settle," Wren said. "Their own population sickened and dwindled until finally there was only a handful left. They could no longer keep out all those who wanted to come. They knew they would have to give up what they loved most in order to save it."

"But if they'd just allowed colonizers to come, they could have kept their planet," Anakin pointed out.

"Yes, but they chose not to. The beauties of their world were too important to them," Obi-Wan explained. "To keep the planet unspoiled was their first goal."

"They sound selfish to me," Anakin said. "They

wanted to keep their planet beautiful for themselves and a few others."

"Or perhaps they were wise," Obi-Wan said. "It is not for us to say."

Anakin turned his gaze back to the planet's surface and sighed under his breath. One of the hardest things he found about becoming a Jedi was suspending judgment. To Anakin, things were good or bad, smart or stupid. Obi-Wan had this maddening way of not taking a stance on things.

"If I had a planet that was truly my homeworld, I wouldn't give it away. I'd want to be able to come back whenever I wanted," Anakin said. He had spent his early years on Tatooine, but he had been a slave. He did not feel as though the planet was his home, even though his mother still lived there.

"The Temple is your home," Obi-Wan said gently.

Anakin nodded, but he knew that in his heart he did not feel that way. He loved the Temple and was always glad to return to it. He loved its order and its grace. He loved the beauty within it, the Room of the Thousand Fountains and the deep green lake. But it did not feel like home.

Unlike the other Jedi students, Anakin had once had a home. Unlike them, he remembered his mother. He remembered running home through the heat and bursting through the door to be met with cool and shade and open arms. He remembered his warm cheek against her cool one . . .

No, his home had not been a planet. It had been smaller, and humbler, and much more precious.

Life in that home had not been easy. There had been times of food shortages, times when they had shivered at night for want of fuel.

The Temple was never short of food or fuel. The temperature was maintained at the optimum degree for the various beings who lived within. It was warmer and safer than the slave quarters on Tatooine.

But it still didn't feel like home. *Home will always be where Mom is. No matter how old I get. No matter how long it's been since I've seen her.*

"There are the Rost Mountains," Wren said. "We'll land and I'll say good-bye there." He grinned over his shoulder at Anakin. "And then you'll try to catch me."

Wren was an older Jedi with a graying beard who had chosen to teach at the Temple rather than continue to go on missions. Anakin had studied the politics of governments with Wren, and he knew the Jedi Master had a wide-ranging grasp of political philosophies in the galaxy. As part of his Jedi service, Wren also volunteered to take part in training missions for Jedi teams.

Anakin and Obi-Wan would try to track Wren through the wilderness. The exercise was designed to strengthen the bond of trust between Master and Padawan. On

Ragoon-6, they would have only each other to depend on as they tracked Wren through the rugged terrain.

Anakin's eyes danced as he bowed respectfully to Wren. "It will be my honor and pleasure to find you in a single day, Wren."

"Ah, in only one day, you say. You are almost as cocky as your Master used to be," Wren said. "I think my clues just got harder. I enjoy teaching lessons to overconfident Padawans."

Anakin hid his grin. In his classes, Wren had been respected, but he'd also been teased behind his back by the Jedi students for taking himself a little too seriously. Anakin would love to find him before a single day had passed. That would deflate his superior manner a bit!

Still, Anakin couldn't help wondering why Obi-Wan had decided to take him on this training exercise. He already trusted his Master with his life. They had been on difficult missions together. He had known him since he was a boy. Every mission brought them closer. Why did they have to take a detour for what seemed to be an elaborate game?

They skimmed over a meadow lush with wildflowers and tall green grass. Above the grassy field, snow-capped mountains hugged the tiny meadow. The sky was deep blue streaked with violet. Anakin could almost smell the fresh scent of the flowers. He had never seen such a lush world with so many vivid colors.

Wren landed the craft expertly in a sheltered spot tucked into the rocky side of the mountain. He accessed the landing ramp and turned to them. "Remember, you must leave your comlinks aboard ship. No homing devices or droids can be used. You must rely on each other and the Force."

Anakin and Obi-Wan nodded. They both knew these things, but it was part of the ritual that Wren repeat them. They placed their comlinks in Wren's hand, and he stowed them in the secure storage bin.

"If you can't find me, we will meet back here in ten days." Pausing only to sling a survival kit over his shoulder, Wren nodded a good-bye. "May the Force be with you." His gray eyes twinkled. "You'll need it."

Wren ran lightly down the ramp. He swung himself up on a flat rock, then jumped to another. Within moments, he had disappeared.

"Wren is certainly looking forward to puzzling us," Obi-Wan observed.

"He really should get out more," Anakin said.

Obi-Wan turned to Anakin. "Do you think Wren is taking this too seriously?"

"No," Anakin said hesitantly. "But I don't understand why a Jedi Knight would want to spend his time this way when he could be on missions."

"Wren has been on hundreds of missions," Obi-Wan said with a frown. "He has served for most of his life.

Now he wishes to give back his knowledge to the Padawans. It is a noble gesture."

Noble, but boring, Anakin thought.

He thought it better not to share the thought with his Master. "How long do we give him?" he asked instead.

"Just a few hours," Obi-Wan answered. "Time enough for us to explore the surroundings a bit and have a meal, you'll be glad to hear. We'll be on rations and protein cubes once we leave, but we can raid the ship's galley now." Obi-Wan gave Anakin a piercing look. "This is designed to teach us, Anakin. But it is also supposed to be fun."

"Of course, Master." Anakin didn't want Obi-Wan to think he wasn't looking forward to the exercise. He knew Obi-Wan had been here twice with Qui-Gon and treasured the memory. Anakin wanted to have that same experience with his Master.

Obi-Wan heated up a meal for them, which they ate sitting in the meadow surrounded by flowers. The morning sun was a brilliant yellow, casting its warmth on Anakin's skin. He ate quickly, anxious to start the day.

"Qui-Gon and I tracked a Jedi named Winso Bykart," Obi-Wan said, pushing aside his plate and leaning back on his elbows. "It was our second trip to Ragoon-6. On the first trip, we had to cut the exercise short. I didn't know why at the time, but Qui-Gon had received a disturbing vision about Tahl."

"I have heard about her," Anakin said. "She was supposed to be brilliant."

"She was. Brilliant and funny and kind. She was unique." Obi-Wan looked out over the meadow. "She was a great friend of Qui-Gon's. I don't know if he ever truly accepted her death."

"But a Jedi must accept death," Anakin said. "It is part of life."

"Yes," Obi-Wan said quietly, his gaze still far away. "That was the difficulty for Qui-Gon."

What do you mean? Anakin wanted to ask. But something stopped him. Sometimes, when Obi-Wan spoke of his Master, he became distant. Anakin could tell by the expression on his face. He did not want to intrude by asking prying questions.

Silence fell between them. Anakin was used to that. Usually their silences felt comfortable. This one was not. Anakin watched Obi-Wan's face. He saw the quiet yearning there. Obi-Wan was missing Qui-Gon. And for the first time, it bothered Anakin.

He wasn't feeling jealous of Qui-Gon, Anakin told himself. It wasn't that. He had loved Qui-Gon, too. Something else was bothering him about his Master's preoccupation.

Maybe it was because he was still envious of their relationship. Obi-Wan had taken Anakin on as his Padawan with reluctance. Anakin had always sensed that.

Qui-Gon had believed in him, and Qui-Gon's belief had influenced Obi-Wan. How could Obi-Wan ignore his beloved Master's dying wish?

Anakin had thought himself lucky at the time. To arrive at the Temple already chosen by a Jedi Knight! It was unheard of.

Now that he was fourteen, he had seen his fellow Jedi students wait and hope to be chosen by a Jedi Knight. He had talked to his new friend, Tru Veld, about it. Tru had told him about how his Master, Ry-Gaul, had studied him. Tru had felt Ry-Gaul's eyes on him during lightsaber matches, during classes, even walking around the Temple. They had shared many conversations together. When Ry-Gaul had officially chosen Tru at last, he had felt honored.

Anakin too had always felt honored to be Obi-Wan's Padawan.

But why? Anakin suddenly wondered. *Obi-Wan did not choose me.*

Today, for the first time, Anakin saw the difference.

Then a new thought pierced his heart. Had Obi-Wan brought him here as a desperate act, to develop a closeness he did not feel?